Apollo never minds his own business. What would be the fun in that? He's the god of the sun, and people are usually happy to see him — but never Set. No, Set looks tempted to strangle Apollo every time they spend time together, and Apollo loves that.

Set doesn't know what to make of Apollo. The sun god is annoying and clingy, no matter how hard Set tries to push him away. When Apollo decides to move in with the Egyptian pantheon — in Set's suite of all places — Set has a hard time keeping him at arm's length.

But no matter how hard Apollo tries to get into Set's pants, the final fight looms on the horizon. Apophis is threatening to end the human realm and the Egyptian pantheon. Set, Ra, and their allies need to face their greatest challenge.

And risk everything to save themselves and humanity.

Greatest Challenge
Copyright © 2024 Catherine Lievens
ISBN: 978-1-4874-4171-5
Cover art by Angela Waters

Published by eXtasy Books Inc

Look for us online at:
www.eXtasybooks.com

# GREATEST CHALLENGE
# FOR THE GODS' AMUSEMENT 7

## BY

## CATHERINE LIEVENS

# CHAPTER ONE

Set was annoyed. As the god of violence, he should have enjoyed the mess Apophis was making, but he didn't. There was such a thing as too much violence, and they'd reached that point a while back.

It wasn't just violence and chaos anymore. It was death and pain, a struggle for power, and an annoyance. Why hadn't Apophis stayed in the underworld? Set didn't understand why he wanted to take over the human world so badly.

Humans could be ingenious, and some of them had an eye for art, but most humans were annoying. They always bothered Set when they found out who he was, and they kept bowing at him and currying for favors. That was why he spent most of his time either in his suite at the palace shared by the gods of his pantheon or in the apartments he had all over the world.

Well, the ones he had left.

Set scowled at the TV. He didn't enjoy watching it and thought it was stupid, but it was the best way to stay informed about what Apophis was up to. At last count, he'd already destroyed two of Set's apartments, and Set didn't like that. He'd selected the places he'd purchased carefully, and he was losing them one by one because Apophis was throwing a temper tantrum.

The human realm was a bother, but it was a bother Set didn't want to lose. As annoying as humans could be, it would be inconvenient to lose the ability to buy their designer suits and delicious alcohol. That meant he'd need to save humanity from Apophis.

Which was why he was expected at a meeting in half an hour. He sighed and got to his feet. He could stay here, but Ra would look for him, so he might as well go. Set's grandfather could be as annoying as the humans he was trying to save, especially since he'd met his partner.

Set found it hilarious that Ra, of all gods, had chosen to be with a god who belonged to another pantheon, but he loved watching how the others reacted to that. None of them would ever say anything to Ra, considering he was the main god in their pantheon, but Set found the deep disappointment and scorn they visibly felt amusing. It was one of the main reasons he liked Frey.

His presence bothered people that Set didn't like.

Set kept the TV on as he went to his bedroom to change. He enjoyed black suits, so he selected one before heading to the bathroom to shower quickly. He wasn't happy about being stuck in the palace with all the other gods. He enjoyed his apartments in the human realm because there, he was alone and didn't have to deal with everyone else. Unfortunately, it wasn't safe to leave the palace until they got rid of Apophis.

Which meant Set had to do so as soon as possible.

Unfortunately, Apophis was powerful. Set wouldn't be able to take him on his own, no matter how much he wished he could. Ra hadn't been able to do so the first time around, either. As annoying as it was, they would have to fight Apophis together.

It didn't take Set long to get ready, and once he was, he turned the TV off and headed out. They were meeting in Ra's rooms, and Set wondered who would be there. They still didn't know who the spy was, which made having meetings to talk about their next steps inconvenient. If the spy was one of them, they would go to Apophis and tell him everything that had been said. That was why they kept their meetings as small as possible, but they'd need all the help they could get to defeat Apophis, which meant involving everyone available.

Set had never trusted anyone but himself, and he had no intention of starting anytime soon. He'd work with Ra and the others because he had to if he wanted to get rid of Apophis, but that was where it ended. He wanted nothing else to do with them.

Most of the people had already arrived when he reached Ra's room. He sat on one of the chairs, leaning back as he looked around. This meeting seemed to be among the gods Ra trusted the most, but there were a few humans present, too. Not all of them were alive, which wasn't a surprise since Osiris was here. He and Thoth had fallen in love with two dead humans, and both of them were here today.

"Have you seen what Apophis has done?" Ra asked as he looked around the room.

Set sighed. He'd hoped something new would come out of this meeting, but he could already tell that wouldn't happen. It made him wonder why they were even meeting. There was nothing new to talk about except what Apophis was doing, and they didn't need to talk about that. They all knew he was destroying the human realm. He wanted full power over humans, and if they refused to bow down to him, he killed them. To him, it was as simple as that.

"Do we really have to make a list of everything Apophis has destroyed since the last time we met?" he drawled.

The conversation stopped, and everyone turned to look at him.

He wasn't bothered by the attention. He'd come all the way here to find a solution to the Apophis problem, not to wail about the people Apophis was killing.

"Don't you want to know what he's been up to?" Sekhmet asked.

"Not particularly. I want to know where he is so we can get rid of him permanently, but I don't need to know what he's been up to."

Sekhmet snorted. "Why are you even here? It's clear you don't care about any of this."

"I do care. I don't want the human realm to be destroyed. It would be annoying."

"Annoying?" Tefnut asked. "How can you talk about human beings like that?"

"None of you cared about human beings until Apophis got free. You stayed up here in your palace, watching the humans under you, not caring about them one bit. It changed because you're afraid that Apophis is going to turn to you after he's done killing them, not because you care."

Sekhmet got to her feet. "How dare you?"

She'd always had an easily triggered temper. Usually it ended in blood, which would be more entertaining than what was happening now.

Ra put a hand on his daughter's shoulder. "Enough, both of you," he said.

She obeyed and settled back on her chair, but Set wouldn't be so easily pushed down. "I understand the need to get rid of Apophis, and I want that as much as you do," he said. "But having all these meetings is useless. We are still no closer to finding a way to kill Apophis permanently. We don't even know if it's possible. We only know what happened in the past and that it worked once, and maybe we should stop talking about it and try to do something. We need to stop hiding and attack him head-on."

Ra was already shaking his head. "We're not strong enough to do that. If we attack him, he'll kill us."

Set sighed. Ra could be right. There was no way to know how powerful Apophis had become while he'd been trapped in the darkness. He was quickly recuperating his power and magic, and he didn't hesitate to use them against the humans. With so many of them now agreeing to serve him, he was getting more powerful every day, which meant that every meeting they had was time wasted.

But no matter how many times Set pointed that out, people didn't listen to him. Ra was the guy in charge because he'd been the one who trapped Apophis the first time around, and everyone seemed okay following him. Set wouldn't have a problem with that—not much of a problem, anyway—if Ra was actually doing something, but they were wasting precious time.

And time was the only thing they didn't have enough of.

Every pantheon was messy. Apollo just had to think about his to be sure of that. He'd stopped finding Zeus's antics amusing a while ago, and he was glad to have a distraction provided by the Egyptian pantheon.

He just wished that massive serpent wasn't trying to eradicate human life from the earth.

Apollo liked humans. He was the god of music and poetry, and humans could be extremely creative. They created art dedicated to him, and it pleased him. He didn't want it to stop, which meant that Apophis needed to go.

The problem was that Apollo wasn't a god in the Egyptian pantheon. He wanted to think he'd be able to defeat Apophis, but what did he know? He had no experience when it came to this kind of thing. When a god from his pantheon misbehaved, Zeus took charge. It never ended well for the troublemaker, and Apollo was tempted to ask Zeus to take care of Apophis.

But Zeus would say no. He would say it was none of their business, and he might even be right, but couldn't he see what was happening? Who would create art dedicated to Apollo and the other gods if there weren't any humans left?

Which was why Apollo was on Mount Olympus. He didn't spend a lot of time here, feeling better when he was as far away as possible from his pantheon, but he wanted to talk to his father. He was sure he already knew what his father's answer would be, but it was worth a try. At the very least, it would enable Apollo to say *I told you so* once this mess was over.

He walked into the throne room. It was large, with a ceiling so high it was hard to see, and two arches opposite each other that let people in and out. Zeus's throne was set in the center, with all the others placed around it in a circle. Zeus's was the biggest, which always made Apollo smile, because he wondered if Zeus was trying to compensate for something.

Hera was the first to notice Apollo. She sniffed and looked away, but Apollo made sure to beam at her as he always did when he saw her. He knew how much his existence annoyed her. He and his twin sister were proof that Zeus had cheated on Hera, and if she had her way, they would never darken the throne room with their presence again.

Knowing how much he annoyed Hera made Apollo's smile widen. He was still smiling when he stopped in front of his father's throne. Zeus was sitting there, doing something on his phone.

"Humans invented that," Apollo said.

Zeus looked up. "What?"

"Your phone. Humans created that and the suit you're wearing."

Zeus looked puzzled. "I'm aware of that."

"And you're also aware that they're dying. It doesn't have anything to do with our pantheon for once, but it's going to impact us anyway."

Zeus's expression turned to suspicion. "I know what's happening in the human realm. You don't have to tell me."

"Don't I? Because Apophis is wreaking havoc, and no one is doing anything about it. Do you want the people who created your phone and your suit to die? What will you wear if they do?"

Zeus's eyes narrowed. "Why don't you get to the point? What do you want from me?"

"For you to intervene. The Egyptian pantheon is working to stop Apophis, but they're having little success. There's a spy in their group, and Apophis has allies. He's also quite powerful, but I'm sure you wouldn't have any trouble with him."

Usually, telling Zeus how powerful he was worked. He was like a peacock. He wanted everyone to see how handsome and powerful he was, and he never missed a chance to do so.

Hera touched Zeus's knee. He turned to look at her, and Apollo knew he'd been defeated before he'd even had a chance to fight. Zeus was going to say no.

Apollo had known this would happen, but that didn't mean he wasn't disappointed. The Egyptian pantheon needed their help, and while usually the different pantheons kept to themselves, things had been changing lately. Apollo had seen how the Egyptian god of the sun, Ra, had taken a god belonging to the Norse pantheon as his partner. Loki, who belonged to the Norse, too, spent more time with the Egyptians than he did with his own family.

Apollo could see the advantage of that. Some days he wished he wasn't related to any of the people in his pantheon. He was pretty sure they felt the same way about him.

"Stay out of it," Zeus said in a booming voice that echoed around the room.

"Isn't it to our best advantage to keep humans alive?" Apollo tried. "What will happen if they're not there anymore?"

"We'll create new ones," Hera said with a huff. "What happens to other pantheons isn't our business. Your father has spoken. Stay out of it."

Zeus looked like he wanted to tell her to stop speaking for him, but he didn't. Instead, he nodded. "This has nothing to do with us, and you'd better remember that."

Apollo didn't push, because it wouldn't change anything except make Zeus angrier. Apollo would do this on his own like he'd planned from the beginning. He'd wanted to give Zeus the chance to do the right thing for once, but his father wasn't one for that. If anything, he tended to avoid doing so.

He grinned. "Well, I suppose that means I'm moving out."

Zeus frowned. "What are you talking about?"

"I like humans, and I have no intention of staying out of it. If I have to ally with the Egyptians to help them, I will. I just thought you'd want to be on the right side for once, but I should have known better."

Zeus got to his feet. "How dare you? You are my son, and you *will* obey my orders."

Apollo raised a hand and wiggled his fingers at his father. "Sure. I'll see you when I see you."

He'd never been happier to be able to teleport wherever he wanted in the blink of an eye. It meant he didn't have to listen to his father rant at him for being a disobedient son as if he were a child.

Apollo had never really been a child. He was a god, and he'd had to deal with his father for too long. It was time to step away from the Greek pantheon and do what was right.

Since he'd already known this would happen, his things were packed. He didn't spend a lot of time in his palace on Mount Olympus, so there wasn't much to take. Besides, if he needed anything, he could always buy it.

Provided that the human realm still existed.

He grabbed his bag and teleported away, pulling all his

things along. He knew where he was going, thankfully. He reappeared in the middle of what appeared to be a meeting. Everyone stopped talking as they took him in, but Apollo had never minded being the center of attention.

He dropped his bag and beamed around the room. "Is this a meeting? Were you waiting for me? Well, you don't have to anymore. I have arrived, and I'm pledging my help to you. Whatever you need to defeat Apophis, I'll give it to you."

For some reason, everyone was still staring. They probably couldn't believe he was on their side and ready to help, which was understandable. After all, not only did Apollo belong to another pantheon, but he was also the god of the sun and a bunch of other things that could come in handy against Apophis.

He left his bags where they'd landed and went to sit down. Luckily for him, there was a free spot next to Set.

Apollo flopped down and beamed at the other god. "You don't have to worry about anything. I'm here to help now."

For some reason, Set stared at Apollo as if he were an interesting insect that he was planning on squashing with his designer shoes.

That didn't bother Apollo. He had plans when it came to the handsome god of storms and violence.

But first, he needed to focus on the meeting.


Set knew he'd regret asking, but he couldn't help it. "What are you doing here?"

For some reason, Apollo smiled at him. Smiling was something Apollo seemed to do often. His face might be stuck that way, now that Set thought about it.

"Well, I came to help," Apollo explained as if Set hadn't understood his words the first time around.

"I think we'd all like to know what that means exactly,"

Frey said carefully from his spot next to Ra.

Set nodded at Ra to let him know he was grateful he was taking the lead on this. He never knew how to deal with Apollo, and he didn't want to have to learn. The Greek god was annoying and shouldn't be here, but this wasn't Set's palace, and these weren't his rooms. If Ra wanted Apollo here, Apollo would stay.

"I talked to my father and pointed out that if we wanted *some* humans to survive, we'd need to help you defeat Apophis. He didn't take it well, but I never expected him to. I decided I'd come and help on my own."

"What kind of help do you think you can give us?" Set drawled. "Aren't you the god of music and dance?"

The scorn in Set's voice wasn't enough to dim Apollo's smile. If anything, it widened. "Amongst other things. I'm also the god of archery, healing, and the sun. I'm sure I can be useful."

"Why would you want to help us? You don't belong to our pantheon."

"Neither do Frey and Loki, yet they're here."

He had Set there. The two Norse gods *were* here, and they weren't going anywhere. They would help in the fight against Apophis, which was a good thing because it meant they had an advantage they hadn't had the first time around.

Back then, they'd only been able to rely on themselves. Set and Ra had worked together, along with other Egyptian gods, and they'd managed to defeat Apophis. It hadn't been enough to kill him, but then that wasn't what they'd been trying to do. The world needed balance, and that was what Ra and Apophis were.

But not anymore. Apophis was taking over, and they had to get rid of the darkness. This time, it would have to be permanent. It wasn't something they would have managed the first time around, but maybe this time, considering they were more powerful and had outside help, they could ensure Apophis never returned.

That would have heavy consequences for Set, but he was ready to shoulder them. Ra would need a new god to step in and create balance, and Set was the god of violence. He could provide that balance.

Set got to his feet, startling a few people. He turned to his brother, not wanting Ra to worry.

Not too much, anyway.

"Let me know when you decide it's time to strike. I have no need for useless meetings, so don't bother inviting me if you're not going to start planning the way to defeat Apophis."

Thankfully, Ra was used to Set's moods. He nodded and thanked him for coming, but he didn't try to convince him to stay.

Set wouldn't have.

He walked out of the room, relieved not to feel the heavy stares on him anymore. The problem was that the main reason he'd left the meeting had followed him.

He turned to Apollo. "What do you want?"

Apollo grinned.

Set didn't understand why he was always smiling. There was nothing to smile about. The world was a mess, and if they weren't careful, they would lose this fight.

"I missed most of the meeting, so I decided I might as well miss the rest of it and spend time with you," Apollo offered.

"Why would you want to spend time with me?"

"That's a good question. You're quite abrasive, so I suppose not many people want to spend time with you. What about your family? Do you spend time with them? If your family's anything like mine, I guess you don't, and that's a good thing."

Set turned around and strode down the hallway. He didn't bother answering Apollo's questions. Paying attention to him would only cause him to stick around longer, which was something Set was trying to avoid.

He continued walking until he reached his rooms. Unfortunately, Apollo did the same, and when Set walked into his suite, Apollo was right behind him.

"What are you doing?" Set asked, gritting his teeth and telling himself he had to resist the urge to punch Apollo. The last thing they needed was a fight between pantheons.

"Is this where I'll be staying?" Apollo asked, ignoring Set's question.

"Absolutely not. You're not staying with me."

But Apollo had already vanished down the hallway. Set heard doors opening and closing and Apollo talking to himself.

"This guest room is perfect for me," Apollo called out. "I'll just get my things."

Set had several options. He could tell Apollo to fuck off and never return, but something told him that Apollo wouldn't take no for an answer. The god was awfully pushy — as pushy as he was handsome. He'd ignore Set's request and settle in as if he belonged here, and Set suspected that nothing he could do or say would change that.

So what was the point in trying?

Set could avoid a lot of headaches if he just let Apollo be. He'd be annoying to have around, but Set was used to having annoying people around. His family fell into that group, and he only felt the need to strangle them a few times a day when he spent time with them.

There was no way Apollo was worse than them.

*Right?*

Apollo reappeared. "So, what's the plan?"

"That would be to get you out of my suite."

Apollo rolled his eyes. "I meant with Apophis. I'm pretty sure my father's pissed and won't allow me to come back home until this is over. I'm tempted not to go back at all, but

I'm pretty sure he'll eventually try to drag me back to Mount Olympus."

Maybe Set should call Zeus. He wasn't sure the god would take his call, but he could tell him where Apollo was and maybe even help him by tying Apollo up or something.

Not that he was thinking about Apollo being tied up. Set didn't want to see that in any way, shape, or form.

But he couldn't deny Apollo was handsome. Of course, he was a god, and all gods were beautiful. They made themselves so. It was more than Apollo's beauty, though. He almost shone from the inside, which would make sense, since he was the god of the sun, but so was Ra, and Set had never felt like he should kiss him.

The thought of kissing Ra made him shiver in horror. They were family, and he'd never look at Ra like that. Unfortunately for him, he couldn't stop looking at Apollo in precisely that way.

Set wanted to slide his fingers through Apollo's blond curls and pull him closer to kiss him. He wanted to shut him up with his mouth and ensure he was so distracted he couldn't start rambling about Apophis again. He couldn't help but wonder how Apollo would look in his bed.

Set shook his head. He had no doubt that Apollo would look beautiful there, just like he looked beautiful everywhere else, but that probably wouldn't be enough to shut him up, which was what Set needed from him right now.

"If you're going to stay with me, there are rules," he said as he took off his suit jacket.

Apollo looked Set up and down in a way that made Set want to grab him, although he wasn't sure if it was to punch him or kiss him.

"What rules?" Apollo asked.

"You don't bother me. You can go and talk with everyone else in the palace, but leave me alone. I like space and privacy, and I won't have enough with you here."

Apollo pouted. "I thought you wanted me here."

"There's nothing I've ever wanted less. I'm tolerating you because we need you, but that's where it ends. If you annoy me, I'll kick you out. I don't care where your father drags you after that."

"You'd come and rescue me from Mount Olympus like a knight in shining armor."

Set snorted and walked away, but he couldn't help but wonder if maybe Apollo was right. As annoying as he was, if he needed to be rescued, Set wouldn't hesitate to help, even though he didn't understand why he felt that way.

What did that say about him and how he felt about Apollo?

# CHAPTER TWO

Set wanted to strangle Apollo. It wasn't a new feeling, but so far, he'd managed to resist. He felt that should earn him a statue at the very least, but he didn't think Ra would agree with him.

Apollo had been living in Set's suite in the palace for several days. Set had thought he'd be able to avoid the Greek god and ignore him when they were both at home, but he'd been wrong.

So fucking wrong.

Apollo was everywhere. Set had hoped he'd stick to his room and would only leave it when they had meetings with the others, but of course, that wasn't how Apollo did things. Apollo's presence was obvious in every room except for Set's bedroom, and Set suspected that Apollo was planning to change that as soon as he could.

He looked around his living room. The loud music made the floor vibrate under his feet. He gritted his teeth. He'd known Apollo was the god of music, but he hadn't expected him to listen to it twenty-four-seven.

He also hadn't expected Apollo to be a slob.

Set eyed his coffee table. It was made of glass, but the only segments he could see of its surface were dirty. The rest of the table was covered in stuff that didn't belong to Set, including two dirty plates, a mug that might have once contained coffee, several books, a couple of phone chargers, and a bunch of other objects that Set wanted to blast with his power. He wondered what Apollo would do if he did that. Would he go running to Ra? Set wouldn't be surprised, and since he didn't want that kind of trouble, he decided he needed to be the first to talk to his grandfather.

Luckily, Apollo was nowhere to be seen, even though the music was playing. Set could have looked for him, but for what purpose? He'd already asked Apollo not to do any of this, but either Apollo hadn't heard him, or he'd decided that what he said didn't matter. It was tempting to kick him out, and Set almost had several times, but he reminded himself once again that Ra needed all the help he could get. Apollo was the god of the sun in his pantheon, just like Ra was the god of the sun in his. Their powers were similar enough that Apollo could help in a way no one else could.

Which was the only reason Set hadn't strangled him yet.

He turned around and left the room as quickly as he'd walked in. He felt better once the door to his suite was closed behind him, but he was still angry. He didn't like living at the palace, but Ra had asked that all the gods move back, and Set had agreed. With so much happening in the human realm, it made sense that all the gods needed to be together and ready to act when they had to.

But that meant that Set didn't have any place to run to when he needed peace. With Apollo having moved into his suite, Set was never alone. Even at night, he could hear Apollo moving through the apartment, playing music and making noise. Set was going to go nuts if he didn't do something.

The best thing would be to talk to Ra, which was what Set planned to do. Luckily, since Ra had ordered that most gods stay at the palace, he was there, too. Set was pretty sure he wished he could go back to the home he shared with Frey, but it would have to wait. In the meantime, the two of them were staying in Ra's suite, so that was where Set headed.

Ra opened the door almost as soon as Set knocked on it. He opened his mouth to speak, but Set pushed past him. Frey looked confused and sat up on the couch, but Set didn't give either of the gods time to ask what he was doing there.

He started pacing the length of the living room, ignoring the TV and the images flashing on the screen. "You need to find Apollo somewhere else to stay. I thought we could share living spaces, but it's impossible. He's a slob and noisy, and he's not scared of me. No matter how many times I threaten him, he just smiles and nods and goes back to doing whatever he was doing before. I'm going to strangle him eventually, and we'll be in trouble with the Greek pantheon. I don't think either of you want that to happen, do you?"

Ra arched a brow. "I thought you said you were fine with him staying with you."

Set glared. "I was until I realized the kind of person he is. He leaves dirty plates on every surface of the suite. He doesn't even have to eat, since he's a god! I'm pretty sure he's doing it on purpose to push me into a reaction, but I'm not giving in. I want him out, and I want you to tell him."

"I suspect it would be best if you told him," Ra pointed out. "It's your place, after all, and you agreed to let him stay."

Set threw his hands in the air. "I already talked to him. I told him to stop being so dirty and to lower the volume of his music, but he won't listen. He even sings, for fuck's sake."

"He's a bad singer?" Frey asked.

Set grumbled. "He's not. He's the god of music and poetry, and his voice is quite nice. He's just annoying. He's a guest in my suite. Shouldn't he do what I say? Shouldn't he at least try not to make a mess?"

Set hadn't been paying attention to the TV, but as he turned, he couldn't help but notice the images on the screen. He stopped pacing and focused on that, frowning when he realized what was happening. "He burned the entire country to the ground?"

Ra's expression turned serious. "He did. They refused to

make him their only god, and this was his revenge."

Set swallowed. Everyone knew Apophis was cruel. He wanted power and wouldn't stop for anything to get it. Things had been bad last time, but this felt worse.

"We need to act as soon as possible," he murmured.

Ra nodded. "We do need to hurry."

"What's the plan, then? We've been having a bunch of meetings, but so far, we still don't know where to start."

Ra and Frey looked at each other. Frey rose from the couch and moved to be close to Ra, who wrapped an arm around his shoulders.

Set looked away. He could have all the lovers he wanted, and he did. He'd never found the kind of connection Ra had with Frey, though, not even with his wife. He barely even remembered he was married most days, and he was pretty sure he wouldn't recognize Nephthys if he saw her. They might be married, but they hadn't spent any time together for the past several thousand years. Divorce didn't exist between gods, but it didn't mean they put any value in their marriages.

But Ra put value in the relationship he had with Frey. It was obvious to anyone who saw them together, and while Set might have scoffed at the sight of Ra in love, part of him wondered if he could ever have that.

Set was the god of storms, disorders, violence, and a bunch of other things most people disliked. He was nothing like his grandfather. He was chaos and much closer to Apophis than he was to Ra. Who would want to be with him, especially with what Apophis was doing?

"We need to separate Apophis from his allies," Frey said. "That means finding the spy and taking care of them and of Maahes. Once we do that, Apophis will be weaker. He won't have as much support, and hopefully, that will mean we can defeat him."

That was the right approach. If they wanted to have a

chance to defeat Apophis, they needed to get him as weak as they could. That meant taking away every god who supported him.

Thankfully, there weren't many. That might change in the future if they didn't act, but Set hoped they'd manage to get rid of Apophis before some of the minor gods decided to take a chance and ally with him.

No one had ever said gods were smart, and most of the gods in the Egyptian pantheon weren't. They went with the power, and at the moment, Apophis *was* the power. If they didn't stop him, he'd be even more powerful than Ra, and they'd lose any chance they might have to defeat him.

None of them could allow that to happen. The world wouldn't survive if Apophis became stronger and gained more allies.

It was time to act. Maybe Set could take his frustration out on Apophis and his allies rather than on Apollo, although he suspected he'd always be tempted to strangle the Greek god. He had a way to get under Set's skin that no one else had.

Set didn't plan to examine the reason behind that anytime soon.

Apollo burst into the living room wearing the smallest pair of shorts he owned — and nothing else. He was already smiling at the thought of Set seeing him like this, and he had an answer ready for whatever Set was about to say.

But the living room was empty. Set was nowhere to be seen, and Apollo frowned, wondering where he'd gone. Why hadn't he warned Apollo that he was leaving the suite? Where had he gone?

Apollo pouted. He'd been planning to seduce Set, but it wasn't going great, and he didn't understand why. Usually, people fell over themselves to end up in Apollo's bed, but not

Set. Apollo wasn't used to having to work for it, and while he didn't mind, it would be easier if he knew what to do.

He sighed and turned off the music. Since Apollo didn't know how long it would take Set to return, he didn't want to stay in the living room and wait. Besides, he'd wanted to explore the palace since he'd arrived and now felt like the perfect moment to do so. He was sure that if he asked Set to go with him, Set would tell him to fuck off. Apollo might as well not ask him and see what happened when he returned.

He went back to his bedroom to change. He wasn't sure what people would think of him if they saw him like this, but since he didn't want to be kicked out, he put on a shirt and exchanged his shorts for a pair of jeans. The Egyptian gods seemed a bit stuffy, so Apollo wouldn't be surprised if they decided he was underdressed because he had on a t-shirt, but he wasn't about to put on the white gown he saw many of the gods wear. It wasn't his style.

Set hadn't returned by the time Apollo was ready, so Apollo left the suite. He had no idea where he was going, but hopefully he'd find something to distract him. He'd come here to help the Egyptian gods, but so far, there had been nothing for him to do, and he never did well when he was bored.

He turned a corner and almost slammed into someone. The only reason he didn't was that he threw his hands forward and grabbed the person's arms, but the person squeaked and quickly stepped back. Apollo looked down at the goddess, trying to place her. He knew the most important gods and goddesses in the Egyptian pantheon, but he didn't recognize this one.

He bowed lightly. "I'm sorry about that. My name is Apollo." He needed to introduce himself to the people who didn't know who he was before they decided he was an intruder.

The goddess raised her chin. "I know who you are."

Apollo grinned. "Most people do." The goddess blinked, looking like she didn't know what to say. That was how people usually felt when they spoke to Apollo, so he wasn't offended. "I didn't catch your name."

The goddess hesitated, and for a moment, Apollo didn't think she would tell him who she was. He didn't think it made a difference. He'd probably never talk to her again, but if he was going to stick around, he wanted to know the people around him.

She nodded stiffly. "Tefnut."

Apollo vaguely remembered the name, but he couldn't place it. "It's a pleasure to meet you."

"May I ask what you're doing?"

Apollo waved. "Exploring. Set's quite boring."

She blinked. "He is?"

"He left me all alone, and I don't know where he is. I promise I won't enter anyone's private space. I just don't want to be stuck in Set's suite forever."

"I understand. I thought you were here to help us against Apophis, though."

"I am, but right now, there's nothing for me to do."

She continued to stare, and Apollo wondered what she was thinking. There was still time for her to start screaming that there was an intruder.

"I was surprised to find out that Ra trusts gods from another pantheon," Tefnut said.

"I'm not sure why you were. From what I know, Loki has been spending most of his time here for a while."

"He's been around for a long time, but you haven't. You've only appeared recently, and people wonder why. What help can you be in our fight against Apophis? What are you planning to do?"

Apollo had enough of this interrogation. He didn't want to

be rude, but he had plans to explore the palace, and this conversation wasn't part of those plans. He bowed lightly and stepped away from Tefnut. "I just want to help. So far, I don't know how I'll do it, but I'm sure Ra will find something I can do. Have a good day."

Since she didn't move to leave, Apollo did. He turned and quickly went down the hallway, then turned a corner. He had no idea where he was going, but he knew better than to open doors, so he stuck to the hallways.

Eventually, he found a garden. He could hear people talking, so he stepped out, already smiling.

As a god, Apollo had seen beautiful things over the thousands of years he'd lived, but the garden was incredible. There were plants everywhere, along with fountains, and in several nooks and crannies, statues of the gods. Apollo could see benches and a few tables, which was where he found the people talking.

His smile widened. He could tell these two weren't gods, but he'd seen them at the meeting. From what he remembered, they were dating two of the gods, and he was curious.

He'd dated humans, but never dead humans.

He flopped onto the bench next to one of the men, who arched a brow at him. Apollo just beamed, knowing that his smile always went a long way to making people comfortable around him.

The man rolled his eyes. "Sure. Why don't you sit down?"

Apollo bounced a bit. "Thank you. What were the two of you talking about?"

The man on the other side of the bench offered Apollo his hand. "I don't know if we've ever been formally introduced, but I don't think so. I'm Lance, and this is Barnaby."

Apollo had never understood the need for humans to shake hands, but he knew about the tradition, so he did it. Thankfully, Lance's hand wasn't sweaty or anything like that.

Maybe it was because he was dead. "I'm Apollo."

Barnaby snorted. "We're aware. I'm surprised Set allowed you out of his sight."

"He wasn't in the suite when I left."

"He's going to freak out when he goes back and doesn't find you."

"Probably. If you hear yelling, it'll be him."

Barnaby chuckled. "I understand why he doesn't like you, but it's the same reason I like you. I wasn't sure what to think of you initially, but I think you'll be good for Set. He's way too serious for his own good."

That pleased Apollo. "Unfortunately, I haven't made any progress yet, but I'm sure I will eventually. He's tough."

"From what I saw, he's used to keeping people at arm's length," Lance offered. "It probably has to do with the kind of god he is. It's not easy to be the god of violence."

Apollo wouldn't know, since he was the god of the sun and a lot of good things, but he suspected Lance was right. "Maybe I need to do something to impress him." It might not be easy to be the god of violence, but Set wasn't the kind of person who thought there was anything wrong with that. He wasn't ashamed of who he was. "I just need him to see me as more than a useless god."

"How do you plan to do that?"

Apollo got to his feet. Barnaby and Lance looked alarmed, which was pretty normal when it came to Apollo's ideas. People usually told him he was crazy, but he didn't think he was. "I'm going to defeat Apophis."

"What do you mean?" Barnaby asked.

"Exactly what I said. I'll defeat Apophis, and Set will see that I'm worthy of him."

"Maybe you could just talk to him," Lance offered.

But Apollo had made his decision. If he wanted Set to notice him, he needed to do something big, and what better than to defeat the god everyone was worried about?

He grinned at Barnaby and Lance. "Thank you so very much for giving me this idea. Soon Apophis will only be a memory, and Set will be mine." Apollo needed to go back to his room. He had a few people to contact, and he needed to find Apophis.

It felt good to have a plan. Apollo couldn't wait to see Set's face when he told him Apophis was gone.


A knock on the door made Set scowl. He and Ra were busy talking about Apophis, and they didn't need to be interrupted. He didn't expect Frey and Ra to ignore the knock, though, so he wasn't surprised when Frey got up and went to open.

Barnaby and Lance barged in. Set dismissed them, turning back to Ra, but he couldn't ignore what they were saying.

"We think Apollo has gone to defeat Apophis on his own."

Set snapped his mouth shut. That couldn't be right. Even Apollo couldn't be that stupid, could he?

Set groaned. Of course Apollo could be that stupid. He was an idiot.

"What happened?" he asked as he got to his feet.

Lance shook his head. "I'm honestly not sure. The three of us were talking in the garden, and he said he wanted to impress you. I don't know why he decided that the best way to do that was to defeat Apophis on his own, but that's what he said he'd do before rushing away."

Set frowned. "Why would he want to impress me?"

"You can't tell me you haven't noticed he wants in your pants," Barnaby said.

Set smoothed down his suit jacket. "Why would he have to defeat Apophis to do that?"

"You tell me."

Set glared at the human. "This is ridiculous. Apollo has to know no one can defeat Apophis by themselves, not even a sun god. Ra wasn't able to do so." He moved toward the door. "I have to go after him. He's going to get himself killed."

Ra put a hand on Set's arm. "I think that going after him would be the worst thing to do."

"What are you talking about? You can't want Apollo to get hurt because he's an idiot."

"I don't believe he's an idiot. I doubt he can defeat Apophis, but he's a powerful god. Apophis won't expect him, and he's never fought him. He's never fought anyone from another pantheon, and while I don't expect Apollo to defeat him, this could still be to our advantage."

Lance cleared his throat. "Apophis *has* fought Apollo. Remember that press conference?"

Set did remember the press conference, just like he remembered it hadn't gone well. "You can't expect me to stay back while he gets himself into trouble."

"We don't know what's going to happen. Besides, how can either of you find Apophis? No one knows where he is."

That much was true, and it helped Set feel better, but he couldn't help but think that Apollo would find a way. He always seemed to, even when he shouldn't.

Set didn't want Apollo to die. He shouldn't care about him, because he was annoying and didn't matter, but Set didn't want a war to start with the Greek pantheon.

Or at least, that was the excuse he told himself.

"He's probably going to walk around the palace for a bit and maybe go to the human realm, but I doubt he can find Apophis," Frey said. "He'll stay out of your way for a while, though. Isn't that what you wanted?"

Set nodded stiffly and sat back down. It *was* what he wanted. He wanted Apollo to stay away from him, and it looked like, for now, that was what he'd get. He should be happy about it. Apollo was annoying, a slob, and never shut up. He always had a lot of questions about things Set would never tell anyone, let alone him, and he didn't seem to care when he didn't get answers. Set could have a little peace while Apollo attempted to find Apophis.

Why did that not make Set happier? Why was he worried about Apollo?

Ra wasn't wrong. Apollo might be an idiot, but he was a powerful god in his pantheon, and he was the god of the sun. In his own way, he was the balance for Apophis, just like Ra. They might not belong to the same pantheon, but pantheons mirrored each other. That was why both Apollo and Ra were the gods of the sun.

Apollo would be all right. He always was.

But for some reason, Set didn't quite believe it.


Hermes eyed the house he and Apollo were standing in front of. "Are you sure this is a good idea?"

"I don't see why it shouldn't be. I'm the sun god, and he's the god of darkness and chaos. I should be able to defeat him."

"It's that *should* that bothers me. If even his own pantheon isn't able to defeat him, what makes you think you will?"

Hermes wasn't wrong, and Apollo *was* a little worried. He made sure not to let Hermes notice, though. He didn't want anyone to think he wasn't convinced of what he was doing. "Maybe I don't have to defeat him right away. I could ask him why he's doing what he's doing."

Hermes snorted. "I'm sure that'll go down well. Why do you think he's doing all of this? Because he's an asshole."

Hermes was probably right. Apophis did look and sound like an asshole, and Apollo doubted he'd listen to him. If it was as easy as asking him to please stop throwing a hissy fit, someone would have already done it.

Apollo hadn't known where to find Apophis, but Hermes always seemed to know everything, and as the herald of the gods and protector of travelers, Apollo had been sure he'd be able to tell him where Apophis was.

He'd been right. Hermes hadn't been happy about it, but he'd shown Apollo where Apophis lived.

Apollo wasn't surprised to see it was in a garish mansion. He *was* surprised to find Apophis in the United States, but he doubted Apophis would stay there for long. With his power and everything he was doing, he could have whatever house he wanted in whatever country he desired. This was probably just a pitstop for him.

Apollo cracked his knuckles. "Wish me luck."

"I hope you won't regret this," Hermes said instead.

Apollo hoped the same. He'd made a lot of stupid decisions in his life, and this felt like it might be one of those. He was here now, though, so he might as well get it over with. Hopefully, he'd have something to show Set by the time this was over.

And hopefully, that something wouldn't be his blood and entrails.

Since he wasn't sure where to start, he strode straight to the front door and knocked. He had to wait for what felt like forever before someone opened, and when they did, he understood why it had taken them so long.

The human looked terrified. She stared at Apollo with wide eyes and cowered as if she expected him to hurt her.

Apollo didn't have to ask to know that she didn't like her new boss. He beamed. "Is Apophis in?"

"Yes," the woman said in a whisper.

Apollo gently pushed past her. "Good. I'll find him myself."

Apollo had no intention of exploring the entire house because it was massive, so he just yelled, "Apophis!"

He then stood in the foyer, waiting for the monster to arrive. The woman squeaked and scurried away. The entrance looked a bit like Zeus's palace on Mount Olympus. Whoever had built this house seemed to have used the earth's entire supply of marble. Between that and the gold accents, the entrance was cold. There was no furniture, just doors that opened into the rest of the house and a massive staircase that led upstairs. There wasn't even a carpet.

"I recognize you."

Apollo turned toward the stairs. Apophis was descending, and he was a contrast to the house. The house was all gold and white marble, but Apophis was dark. He wore a dark suit, and his black hair was tied back away from his face. His eyes were entirely black, which was slightly unsettling. He looked a bit like Set, but there was no warmth in his gaze or any of his movements.

"I'm Apollo, from the Greek pantheon," Apollo explained.

"Why are you here?"

"Well, I wanted to ask why you're doing all of this. To me, it doesn't make sense. It's great to have power and all of that, but if you kill half of your followers, it feels a little useless. Humans are more useful than you'd think, and I really believe you should give them a chance instead of killing them."

"You're here to ask me to stop killing humans?"

"I think it would be the best way to do this. If you don't stop, I'll have to fight you."

Apophis arched a brow. "Will you? Well, I have no intention of stopping. In fact, I won't stop until the entire human realm is mine and all the gods have been eliminated." He cocked his head. "Starting with you."

He was fast, but Apollo had expected an attack. When Apophis rushed toward him, Apollo threw a hand in front of himself. His sword appeared, its light blinding. Apollo was used to it, so he had no problem seeing through the light, but

Apophis had to close his eyes.

That didn't stop him. Apollo brandished his sword just as Apophis crashed against him. Apollo had no idea where Apophis had gotten the two long knives he was fighting with, but he didn't think it mattered.

What *did* matter was that Apophis seemed intent on killing Apollo with them.

Apophis pushed away, and Apollo twirled. He raised his sword again, the clash of steel against steel loud in the otherwise empty room. He put a little more power into his sword and slashed at Apophis, but the god of chaos danced out of the way.

Apollo suspected he'd miscalculated. He'd thought he could get rid of Apophis on his own, but from the way Apophis countered his attacks, he was starting to doubt that. Their previous fight had been short, and he'd had help then. He didn't this time.

He might be in trouble.

But he wouldn't allow Apophis to see he was worried. He pushed forward, intent on using his sword against the other god. Even if he could only wound him, he'd be happy.

Apophis feigned right, then tried to attack on the left, but Apollo anticipated him. He managed to slide his sword against Apophis's arm, ripping his black suit. He didn't have time to see if Apophis was bleeding, but he felt smug at the thought that he'd hurt the god.

He heard the sound of someone behind him just in time to twist his upper body. It was the only thing that saved him because the knife had been aimed at his heart. The man who wielded it didn't hesitate even one second, and the knife sank into Apollo's shoulder.

He hissed with pain and raised his sword, pushing the new god away.

Apollo had no doubt this was a god and that he was

Apophis's ally. He knew Apophis had at least one of them, probably more. "I didn't expect you to need help," Apollo taunted. His shoulder hurt, but he'd rather die than show it.

Apophis's eyes narrowed. "I don't need help to defeat you."

"Really? Because to me, it looks like you do. He didn't even attack me from the front. He thought he'd stab me in the back and kill me before I could see him. He's a coward, and I wonder if you are, too."

Apophis screeched and rushed forward with both of his knives aimed at Apollo's heart.

Apollo had had enough of being a pincushion, though, and he quickly teleported away.

He landed in the middle of Set's living room. "That could have gone better," he murmured as he made his sword vanish and turned his attention to his shoulder.

"What the fuck were you thinking?" Set bellowed as he rushed closer.

Apollo blinked. "What happened?"

Set glared. "What happened? Shouldn't I be the one asking you that since you have a knife sticking out of your shoulder?"

"It's nothing. Apophis's guard dog scratched me."

Set sucked in a breath. "We're going to have a long conversation about this kind of behavior, but I'll take care of your wound first."

Apollo could have healed himself in seconds, but Set was offering to do it for him, and he wanted that. Maybe if he played his cards right, his little trip to the human realm would get him what he wanted.

Set's attention.

# CHAPTER THREE

Apollo might have been exaggerating how bad his wound was. Set had healed him in seconds yesterday, but Apollo had complained that he felt faint and needed rest, and Set had rushed to help him to the couch. Since then, he'd been hovering around Apollo, asking him if he needed anything about a thousand times a day.

Apollo loved it.

There was still a little pain in his shoulder, but the wound was healed and hadn't even left a scar. There was no reason for Set to hang around like this and worry about Apollo, and while Apollo should probably tell him that, he didn't want to. He wanted to keep Set's attention. He wanted them to spend a little more time in Set's suite, just the two of them.

They'd have to go back to the real world and what Apophis was up to soon enough. In the meantime, Apollo would take advantage of every second Set was giving him.

"I could really use a snack," he said.

He was sprawled on the couch, watching TV, or at least, he'd been watching TV before being distracted by Set. Set was focused on his phone, frowning and glaring, and Apollo wanted to know who he was texting.

Set looked up. "You're a god. Use your powers to get yourself a snack."

Apollo pouted. "But I'm wounded and in pain. You can't expect me to get myself a snack. You said you would take care of me."

Set sucked in a breath.

Apollo knew he'd been pushing his patience, and it probably wasn't a great idea, but he was having fun. Set wasn't avoiding him anymore, and he took Apollo's teasing without even threatening him.

A plate of pastries appeared on the coffee table. Apollo beamed and leaned forward to snatch a croissant.

"I thought your shoulder hurt," Set pointed out.

Apollo made a show of gingerly touching the spot where he'd been stabbed. "It does. Do you think that maybe the blade was poisoned? Am I slowly dying?"

Set rolled his eyes. "You're not slowly anything. I don't think you've done anything slowly in your entire life."

Apollo wiggled his eyebrows. "I can be slow if I want to."

Set looked away, but if Apollo wasn't mistaken, he'd seen a slight redness to his cheeks. It might just be Apollo's imagination, but it made his heart soar.

He knew Set wasn't as annoyed and bothered by Apollo as he acted. It would have been easy for him to heal Apollo and kick him out or to have someone else heal him. Apollo had suggested asking the god of medicine, but Set had glared at him and told him to shut his mouth. Set might not say it out loud, but he cared.

Apollo was starting to realize that he couldn't expect words from Set, but he only had to watch Set's actions to know what he was feeling. He was taking care of Apollo, even though they both knew Apollo was healed and felt no pain. For some reason, though, Set was going along with this, and Apollo hoped it was because he liked Apollo and wanted to spend more time with him.

"I still don't understand what you were thinking, going to Apophis like that," Set said.

Apollo swallowed his mouthful of croissant—almond croissant, his favorite—before answering. "I don't think I was thinking much, to be honest."

Set snorted. "Something tells me you don't often think."

"Not if I can avoid it." He took another bite of pastry and sighed. "I guess I wanted to understand him. I don't know why he's doing this, and I have a hard time believing that power is his main motivation. The more humans he kills, the less power he has over the human race. Besides, why would he want to kill so many of them? I like humans, and they're useful."

"I don't know about useful," Set grumbled.

"Oh, stop it. We both know you like humans well enough to wear their clothes and eat their food."

"You're the one eating, not me."

Apollo pushed the plate with the pastries toward Set and stared at him until Set huffed and grabbed one of them. He chose a *pain au chocolat*—a plain exterior with a sweet center. Apollo wondered if that said anything about him. Even though Set was a god of violence, storms, and a bunch of inconvenient things, he was sweet when he wanted to be.

The problem was that he didn't often want to be.

"I think that more than power, what Apophis wants is chaos and pain," Set said.

He was staring at his pastry after only taking one bite. Apollo wanted to tease him, but Set had turned serious, and Apollo wanted to hear what he had to say.

"He's the god of chaos, after all," Set explained. "And he's been locked up for thousands of years. I imagine he's been resentful the entire time, and now he wants to make people pay."

"He's focusing on the wrong people, then. He should be trying to make you and Ra pay, not the human realm."

"But we have protection. I don't know if we'll win this fight, but we have allies we didn't have last time. I'm sure Apophis is aware of that, which is why he hasn't attacked us head-on. He will eventually, but first he's going to hurt us through the human realm."

"He can't think that will work with you." Even though it would. Set might act as if he didn't care about anyone or anything, but Apollo knew it was just an act. Set didn't want the human realm to be destroyed any more than Apollo did. He just acted like he didn't care.

"Maybe not with me, but with Ra? He's always had a soft spot for humanity, and that hasn't changed."

"So Apophis is torturing Ra and, at the same time, making himself more powerful by creating more chaos," Apollo said.

Set nodded. "Exactly. All this chaos and pain are making him stronger."

Apollo shook his head. "I still don't understand."

"That's the difference between you and gods of chaos and pain. You don't think like we do. You don't want the same things we do."

Apollo frowned. "Why are you including yourself in that group?"

"Because I'm the Egyptian god of violence. What do you think that means?"

"You might be the god of violence, but it doesn't mean you're happy about what Apophis is doing. In fact, I know you're not. You want to stop him as much as we all do." Apollo was sure of that, and he didn't need Set to tell him.

He didn't care what kind of god Set was. He was on their side, working to save humanity from Apophis's chaos, and that was all that mattered. Who cared what Set was the god of as long as he was good?

And he *was* good. Set might be gruff and sharp around the edges, but that was only a façade. Apollo could see under that exterior, and he liked what he found. He wanted to get to know Set even better, and luckily, Set was finally allowing him in.

Set got to his feet. "You don't know what you're talking

about. You don't know me."

Apollo smiled. "Not yet."

"Why would you want to get to know me? I'm rude, and no one likes me."

"*I* like you."

Set stared. He looked like he didn't understand what Apollo was saying, or rather, that he couldn't understand why Apollo felt that way. Sometimes Apollo himself didn't understand, but he didn't need to.

He saw Set in a way many people didn't. Being a god himself, he could see beyond what Set was supposed to be to the man he actually was. Set might be a god, but that didn't mean there wasn't humanity in him.

Apollo saw how important stopping Apophis was to Set. He might tell himself it was for selfish reasons, but Apollo didn't think that was entirely it. Of course Set wanted Apophis to be gone so he could go back to his old life, but he also didn't want thousands of human beings to die for no reason. He wouldn't let chaos and violence win, even though he was their god.

In Apollo's eyes, that made him a better god than most.

Set was aware Apollo wasn't staying with him just to bother him. If that was all he'd wished to do, he could have found another way. No, he'd wanted to stay with Set because he liked him.

Set didn't understand that.

He wasn't likable. Even most gods in his pantheon gave him a wide berth. They were afraid of him because he was the god of violence, and he'd always played into that. Having people stay away from him meant that no one bothered him, which he enjoyed because most people were fools, but sometimes, it was a bit lonely.

It was impossible to feel lonely with Apollo around.

Apollo was too good for this world. He might be annoying, but deep inside, he was a good person. He'd never held who Set was against him. He didn't care that Set growled more than he talked or that he looked like he was about to kill someone every half hour. Set didn't know how Apollo could see right through that to the real him, but it made him uncomfortable.

A lot of things about Apollo made Set uncomfortable, including the fact that he was annoying as fuck. Luckily for Apollo, he was also pretty and charismatic, which meant that people tended to want to spend time with him anyway.

Including Set.

That was why Set should be careful. He needed to stay away from Apollo, because once all of this was over, Apollo would realize he could have so much better and leave.

He'd be right to leave. No matter what Apollo thought, Set wasn't a good person, and he'd never claimed to be. He couldn't be a good person when he was the god of violence. He was god of other things, too, but violence was the only one most people remembered.

Set didn't want to stain Apollo with it. He was the god of the sun, and it would be too easy to pull him into the darkness.

Set got to his feet.

Apollo blinked at him, as if he didn't understand what was happening.

Set didn't know, so he didn't have answers for Apollo. "I'm not good," he said with a growl.

Most people would have scurried away, but not Apollo. He continued eating his pastry, looking like he belonged on Set's couch. "That's what you try to convince people of."

Set wasn't surprised that Apollo was a stubborn asshole, but surely even he could see that Set was right. "You do remember which god I am, right?"

Apollo raised his fingers as he made a list. "Well, you're the god of storms, of foreigners, of the deserts, oh, and of storms."

He was right. Most people got stuck on the fact that Set was the god of violence and disorder, but not Apollo. He'd looked deeper, and he'd found more. "I'm also the god of violence," Set reminded him.

Apollo rolled his eyes. "So? If you think that's enough for me to stay away, then you don't know me."

"It should be enough. We don't belong together. I'm dark, and you're light."

Apollo grinned. "I do see we're different, but I don't think that's a problem. I'm also very excited by the fact that you think about us together. I would rather you not believe we don't belong, but it's a step forward and better than nothing."

How could a man be so infuriating? "You know who I am, so why would you want to spend any time with me? Why are you still here, in my suite?"

Apollo had finished eating. He licked his fingers one by one as he stared at Set, and Set forced himself not to look away. Did he find Apollo incredibly sexy? Yes. How could he not when Apollo was licking his fingers like that? But Set was an extremely old god, and he'd seen and done everything there was to see and do in the human realm. One little sun god wouldn't be enough for him to run or to feel ashamed of what he felt.

Apollo rose to his feet, and Set was glad for the coffee table between them. He wasn't sure what Apollo would do if it wasn't there, but he wasn't eager to find out.

"I know the Egyptian pantheon is older than the Greek one, but surely you're not so old that you don't remember what I told you earlier already," Apollo teased. "I like you, Set. I don't have a reason to, and I don't need one. I just know that

I like you and want to spend more time with you. I realize we have to solve the Apophis problem, but once that's over, you won't be able to get rid of me."

That sounded like a threat, but Set's body and heart didn't think that way. He wanted to pull Apollo into his arms and shut him up with his lips. He wanted to drag him to his bedroom and not let him leave for several days.

That would be the worst thing they could do, so Set shook his head. "Even if Apophis wasn't a problem, it still wouldn't make sense for us to be together."

As always, Apollo wasn't deterred. He beamed as if Set hadn't just turned him down, and Set could only stare.

"That's what you think, but I always get what I want, and what I want right now is you. You should give in, but even if you don't, it doesn't matter." Apollo winked. "I like the chase."

# CHAPTER FOUR

They'd been called to another meeting, and it took all of Set's self-control not to scream.

Were so many meetings necessary? They already knew what they needed to do. They had to find the spy, get rid of them and Maahes, and attack Apophis. It was easier said than done, and Set couldn't deny that, but it didn't mean they needed to talk about it time and time again.

"I'm still in pain," Apollo declared from the couch.

They both knew it was a lie. Even if it wasn't, his pain would be in his shoulder.

Set glared at him. "I don't understand why that means I should carry you to the meeting. I wasn't planning to go, anyway."

Apollo gasped. "We can't skip the meeting. Ra needs our help. And think about what everyone will say if we both skip it! Do you want your pantheon to think you're sleeping with me?"

Set rolled his eyes. "I'm pretty sure at least half of them already believe that."

Apollo frowned. "Only half? I'll have to work harder."

Apollo shouldn't be so adorable, but he was. Most of the time, Set didn't know how to deal with him, and today wasn't any different. He'd been sure he'd heard Apollo wrong when Apollo had declared that Set would need to carry him to the meeting, but he hadn't. Apparently, getting stabbed in the shoulder meant that Apollo's legs didn't work anymore.

"Anyway," Apollo continued as he raised his arms and

wiggled his fingers. "You'll carry me, and I'm sure everything will be fine."

"You were stabbed in the shoulder," Set pointed out.

"I remember where I was stabbed. I can still feel the pain of the cold blade sliding into my flesh. I'm still not entirely sure the knife wasn't poisoned, by the way."

Set pinched the bridge of his nose. He told himself that he couldn't kill a god from another pantheon. It would create too much trouble, and they already had enough of that with Apophis. Maybe once Apophis was defeated? Set was pretty sure Apollo would always be infuriating, so it was something to keep in mind.

"It wasn't poisoned, and I healed you almost right away. You've been using this as an excuse to spend your days on the couch, and I don't care about that beyond the fact that you're a slob who can't clean up after himself, but this is too much. I'm not carrying you to the meeting."

Set could imagine everyone staring at him and Apollo. Ra would probably be amused, but the other gods wouldn't know what to think. They saw Set as darkness and anger, and often they weren't wrong. Set wouldn't mind keeping them on their toes, but that didn't mean he wanted to carry Apollo.

But he did, a little bit.

If anything, it would make Apollo shut up, which would be perfect. He'd been talking Set's ears off for what felt like forever, and Set yearned for the day Apollo finally shut up. If Set refused to carry him, he'd continue begging and annoying him, so maybe Set should give in.

He eyed the blond. Apollo wasn't the type to hold anything over anyone's head, but Set had no doubt he would remind him of that time he'd carried him to the meeting because he'd been stabbed and was dying. Set didn't think he could live with that.

Set sighed. "I'm going to the meeting."

Apollo was on his feet in seconds. Set turned toward the door but froze when Apollo climbed onto his back. He wasn't heavy, but only because Set was a god. Otherwise, they'd both be kissing the floor right now.

"Thank you," Apollo murmured.

His breath was warm against Set's skin, and the sensation was enough to make Set shiver. What the fuck was happening to him? How could a single god he didn't even like have this kind of effect on him?

Set wasn't sure he wanted to find out. Apollo made him feel unsteady, and he disliked that. He didn't know how to deal with it and more importantly, how to make it stop. Kicking Apollo out might work, but Apollo wouldn't go easily.

"We're going to be late," Apollo said as he squeezed his arms and thighs around Set.

Set moved toward the door. What else could he do? He could dump Apollo to the floor and tell him to stay the fuck away, but what good would that do? Even when Set growled and snapped at Apollo, he never seemed to be afraid. He wasn't intimidated. He took everything with a smile, which wasn't something anyone ever did, and Set didn't know what it meant.

Beyond the fact that Apollo was an annoying asshole, anyway.

Set sighed heavily and left his suite. Apollo continued talking the entire way to Nu's suite. They were meeting there today because Nu had insisted. They were more comfortable in their own spaces, which Set could understand.

The door was open when they arrived, so Set walked straight in. He looked around for a nearby couch or horizontal surface on which he could dump Apollo, but it was too late.

Almost as one, everyone in the room turned to look at them. Set glared, even though he would have been staring at himself if he'd been in their place, too.

He stepped up to the nearest couch and dumped Apollo on top of it. Apollo didn't seem to mind that Set was being a little rough. He looked at him with a smile and quickly squeezed his hand. "Thank you so much." He looked around the room. "I'm in a bit of pain, and Set offered to carry me to the meeting. He's a sweetheart."

Maybe Apollo wouldn't think that once Set strangled him. And what was everyone doing? Why were they still staring?

"Don't we have a meeting to start?" Set snapped.

Ra cleared his throat. "Right. We should get started."

Thankfully, most people were distracted after that. It meant they weren't staring at Set as if they expected him to explode or something. He felt he might after what Apollo had done to him, and he did his best not to look at anyone as he sat in the only empty seat left—next to Apollo.

Unfortunately, this meeting was as boring as the others. He, Ra, and Frey had already talked about the next step, so they knew what was supposed to happen. They just didn't know how to make it happen.

"How weak will he be once we take the spy and Maahes away?" Barnaby asked. "Don't get me wrong, I think it's the right thing to do, but I can't imagine it'll be easy to defeat him anyway."

"It won't be," Ra confirmed. "But sealing away the demons has helped, and this will, too. Besides, we have more allies than we ever did in the past. We have another sun god working with us. Apollo might not know what to do when it comes to defeating Apophis, but he'll be a lot of help."

Apollo perked up. "I will," he agreed.

Set rolled his eyes.

"And I want to go after that guy you're talking about. I think he's the one who stabbed me," Apollo continued.

"Maahes?" Frey asked.

Apollo shrugged. "Maybe. I just saw that he only had one

hand." He wrinkled his nose. "Quite nasty."

"Yet he still managed to stab you," Set drawled.

Apollo stared as if he couldn't quite believe what Set was saying. Set couldn't, either. Was he teasing Apollo? What the fuck was he doing?

Apollo eventually smiled. "Only because he attacked me from the back while I was fighting Apophis. I want revenge for what he did to me."

Set could understand that, and he wouldn't try to stop Apollo. He'd do the same if he were in Apollo's place. "How will you do that when you're still in pain?" he teased.

"Haven't you heard? A true love's kiss will heal anything." Apollo puckered his lips.

Set stared. He didn't understand Apollo even when he made sense, but right now, he didn't, which was confusing. What was Apollo doing? What was he asking for?

"I can kiss you," Nu offered.

A few people in the room snickered. Set quickly glared at them. He couldn't do the same with his grandparent, but he knew they'd only been teasing.

What had the world come to? Why were people who were supposed to fear him and tremble before him teasing him and making fun of him instead?

"I'm really sorry, but you're not my true love," Apollo said with a pout. "I kind of wished you were, though. I'm sure you'd be easier to deal with."

"Focus," Set snapped. "You already fought Maahes, and it didn't end well. Going out there on your own won't do any good. You might even get hurt, which isn't something we can afford. Ra is going to need you soon."

Apollo blinked. "Only Ra?"

Why couldn't Apollo be serious for a moment? Why did he always have to push Set to the end of his patience?

And why did Set like it so much?

Maybe Apollo shouldn't have been so dramatic about his wound. It hadn't hurt since Set had healed him, but Apollo had been taking advantage of having been stabbed in the shoulder to get more attention from Set.

It looked like he might have made a mistake.

He was fine, but the people around him were looking at him as if he was about to break. That meant he needed to show them that he could still help them, defend himself and the human realm, and that he wasn't worried about Apophis or his little guard dog. Killing the asshole who'd stabbed him would help with that.

It would also help Apollo feel better, and that was always a plus.

He was acting lighthearted, but being wounded had hit him hard. He'd gone into the fight expecting to struggle a bit but eventually win, and instead, he'd come home with his tail between his legs. He was lucky no one had told him how much of a dumbass he was, but he knew that was what they were all thinking, and he couldn't blame them.

He *was* a dumbass.

He'd been trying so hard to impress Set, and instead, he'd shown him that he wasn't good enough. That was why he needed to do this. If he killed Maahes, or at the very least, captured him, Set would know he wasn't weak and that he could help protect him and his pantheon.

Not that Set needed protection. He'd probably snarl and bite Apollo's head off if Apollo ever suggested something like that, so he wouldn't.

What he *would* do was go after Maahes. Apollo might not have been able to defeat Apophis, but they weren't talking about Apophis here. They were talking about his minion.

"We can't afford to lose you when you could make the

difference between winning and losing," Set said gruffly. "That's the only reason I'm worried."

Apollo could tell it was a lie, but he didn't call out Set in front of everyone else. Set was visibly uncomfortable and probably wanted nothing more than to run away, and Apollo wished he could give him that. For now, though, they were both stuck in this meeting, and they had to make the most out of it.

"How about you come with me?" Apollo offered. "You'll have to stand far enough away that Maahes won't try to use you against me, but I'm sure I can defeat him easily, especially if you're watching me." Because he wanted to impress Set.

"Why should I be watching you?"

Apollo wiggled his eyebrows. "How about because you want to?"

Set stared at him like he didn't know what to make of him.

If he was honest, Apollo didn't know what to make of himself on most days. He leaned forward. "If you're so worried about me, you really should come with me. I'm going either way, so think about it."

"If I can't stop you from going, I'll have to go with you. I feel that if I don't, you'll ruin everything and probably make half the human realm explode or something. We can't afford that, and I don't want to have to explain to your father that you died because you were an idiot."

Apollo grinned. "My father would probably make you a statue in the throne room if you were to tell him I was dead." Apollo thought a statue of him looking his best would be better, but if he was dead, he wouldn't care.

Probably.

"I don't need any statues. I just don't want you to make a mess."

Apollo bounced a bit. "Does that mean we're going to work together? That we're a team? We should come up with a name. I like how those people in the superhero movies have a collective name."

"We don't need a name," Set said through gritted teeth.

Apollo was unwilling to stop pushing. He enjoyed their bickering and wanted more. Maybe one day, he'd push Set so far that Set would throw him on the nearest flat surface and punish him. "Fantastic duo? Oh, or maybe a play on the fact that you're dark and I'm light. How about sun dark? Dark sun? I quite like that one."

"I thought you were supposed to be the god of poetry," Set grumbled.

"I'm sure I can do better. Just give me a few more days."

Ra cleared his throat. "Apollo, are you sure it's a good idea for you to go after Maahes? We can send someone else."

"I'm fine." Apollo rolled his shoulders to show Ra he wasn't lying. "Set was the best nurse I could have asked for and healed me perfectly."

"Not a nurse," Set grumbled. "And if you're healed, why did you have me carry you all the way here?"

"Because it was fun." Apollo leaned closer and kissed his cheek. "I can't wait to do it again, but maybe next time, I should carry you."

Set looked like he might bite Apollo's face off if he ever tried anything like that, and since Apollo needed his face and quite liked it, he wasn't willing to try it now. One day, though.

"Maahes won't know what to make of Apollo," Nu said. "I feel it's a good idea to have him go. Everyone knows Loki, but Apollo and even Frey are still unknown. Apophis will be curious to see what they're up to, but he might not expect them to fully step into the fight. Frey has a reason to since he's with Ra, but Apollo doesn't, and it might be enough to give us the element of surprise."

Apollo beamed. "Maahes won't know what hit him."

But Apollo wouldn't be surprised Set was what hit

Maahes. He looked ready to hit someone, but since he'd never hurt anyone who didn't deserve it, he'd have to wait until they got their hands on Maahes to let out a little steam. Apollo would offer that they could do so in a different way, but he didn't fancy being rejected in front of a crowd.

"I hate all of you," Set said. "But if he's going, I'll go with him."

Apollo grinned. He'd be able to show Set that he was a good partner and that he could protect him. That was what he'd been trying to do when he'd gone after Apophis, but this would work even better. Set would be there to see just how strong Apollo was. After Apollo defeated Maahes, Set would fall into his arms. He might even apologize for being all snarky and not believing that Apollo could defeat Maahes.

Apollo couldn't wait.

# CHAPTER FIVE

Apollo was ready to take on the world — or, as it was, one little Egyptian god. He'd asked for information on Maahes, so he knew the man was a minor god. For someone like Apollo, it should be easy to get rid of him. The only reason Maahes had managed to hurt Apollo before was that he'd attacked him from behind, and Apollo wouldn't let him do that a second time.

He was ready to fight.

"We can go now," he told Set as he watched him read the news on his phone.

For all that Set insisted he didn't care about the human realm and that he hated the news, he spent a lot of time checking in on humanity. Apollo thought his grumpiness and the way he obviously cared were adorable.

The meeting had lasted a few hours, but nothing important had happened. Apollo was impatient, so the sooner they got rid of Maahes, the happier he'd be.

Set looked up. "Do you know where to find Maahes?"

"Well, I suppose we could go to the mansion where Apophis lived when I visited him, but if you'd rather not, I can ask Hermes to help."

Set put down his phone and leaned forward. He always looked more relaxed in his suite. He didn't have to keep up pretenses or a mask when it was only him or even when it was only him and Apollo. Knowing that made Apollo's heart flutter. He couldn't believe that Set trusted him enough to show him how soft and squishy he was inside.

"Hermes?" Set asked.

"You know, the Greek god."

Set rolled his eyes. "I know who Hermes is. I just didn't realize he was how you found Apophis the first time around."

"He always knows all the gossip and where everyone lives. It was easy for him to find out, and he took me to the mansion."

"And he didn't think to stay and help you fight?"

"It's not his fight."

Apollo didn't blame Hermes for not helping him. It wasn't really about Apophis but rather about what Apollo's father would do if he found out that Hermes was on his side. Apollo hadn't returned to Mount Olympus since talking to Zeus, but he couldn't imagine things were peachy up there.

They never were.

"It's not your fight either," Set pointed out.

"It *is* my fight. I made it so, and I'm not giving up."

"You're going to get yourself killed."

"Of course not. You'll be there to protect me, won't you?"

Set's expression turned weird for a moment, but before Apollo could worry about what it meant, it vanished. It left behind a scowl.

Apollo beamed.

"You don't need me to protect you," Set grumbled.

"Maybe not, but I *want* you to protect me. Are you ready to go?"

"Where are we headed? Where do you need to go to talk to Hermes?" Set frowned. "Mount Olympus?"

Apollo shook his head and grabbed Set's hand. Set looked like he wanted to jerk away, but Apollo didn't give him time. He teleported both of them to Greece.

Set rolled his eyes when he saw where they were. "Of course."

"We're nothing if not predictable," Apollo said with a

wink. He took out his phone and called Hermes, not at all surprised to hear his phone ring somewhere in the distance.

They were in a small abandoned temple, and it looked like no one was there, but Apollo knew his family. He knew Artemis the best since she was his twin, but he'd made a point of keeping tabs on everyone. Hermes had built a small house behind the temple that was dedicated to him, and when he wasn't on Mount Olympus or out doing favors, this was where he could be found.

"You better answer your phone," Apollo called out.

Someone swore, making Apollo's smile widen. Hermes appeared from between the olive trees, only to stop when he saw Set. He had to have met gods from other pantheons before, but Set was a sight to behold, so Apollo didn't blame him for being stunned.

"What are you doing here?" Hermes asked, still eyeing Set. "I'm surprised you're alive."

"I'm fine, but I need you to find someone for me."

Hermes turned his full attention to Apollo. "Please tell me you're not stupid enough to go after that god again?"

"I won't tell you anything, then."

Hermes groaned. "I don't understand why you're so bent on doing this. It's none of your business. Don't we have enough problems in our pantheon without adding the problems of other pantheons to the mix?"

Apollo pressed his lips together. He understood where Hermes was coming from, but he didn't think anyone truly understood how dangerous this was. "What do you think will happen if Apophis manages to destroy his pantheon? Do you think it will be enough for him?"

Set snorted softly. "He won't stop until he has every god under his heel."

Apollo nodded at Hermes. "Exactly. Once he's done with his pantheon, he'll turn to others. I'm not saying he would win if he attacked my father, but there's a chance he might, and I don't want things to get that far. I'm doing this because it's the right thing to do and because if I don't, we'll end up in trouble anyway. I'd rather stop Apophis as soon as possible."

Hermes sighed. "I get it. So you're looking for him again?"

"I'm looking for a minor god called Maahes. He stabbed me."

"He's living the dream, then."

Set snickered, but Apollo wasn't offended. He knew he was annoying, and he didn't mind if his family teased him, at least when it came from Hermes. He wouldn't have taken it as nicely if Zeus had been the one to say it.

"Give me as many details as you can," Hermes ordered.

Apollo took a step back because Set knew the god they were looking for much better than he did. Thankfully, Hermes was an expert, and after just a few moments, he wiggled his fingers. Apollo gripped them without hesitating, but Set didn't, so Apollo grabbed him.

Hermes took them to a house. This one was smaller, and Apollo wondered if Apophis was annoyed. Clearly, he felt he deserved the biggest and most luxurious things he could find in the human realm, but he didn't seem to have realized that without humans, he wouldn't get them.

"The god you're looking for is in there," Hermes said. "I'm going to Mount Olympus. If you need help, you know how to find me."

Apollo nodded and watched Hermes vanish before he turned back to the house. It might not be as luxurious or big as the other one, but Apollo wouldn't mind living there.

He stepped forward but didn't go far before a hand on his arm stopped him. He turned to Set, who looked confused but quickly set his expression. "Be careful," he ordered.

Apollo's heart fluttered. "I knew you cared about me."

"I never said I cared about you. I just don't want to have to deal with your pantheon before we're rid of Apophis."

Apollo didn't believe him. He thought it obvious that Set cared about him, even though Set would never admit it out loud. It didn't matter. Eventually, Apollo would get what he wanted because he could tell that Set wanted the same.

Set was used to keeping everyone away and hiding his heart from every single person who tried getting close to him. Apollo would be surprised if anyone tried anymore, actually. Apart from Ra and a few other gods, most gods in the Egyptian pantheon seemed to avoid Set as much as they could. That made Apollo angry, but he also understood that it was partly Set's fault. If he didn't growl and snap so much, people would want to spend more time with him. At the same time, all of his growling was a shield for him and a way to keep people as far away as possible so they wouldn't hurt him. Apollo didn't know why Set had started doing that, but he didn't think it mattered. It was over, anyway. Apollo didn't care if Set didn't talk to any of the gods in his pantheon ever again as long as he let Apollo in.

It would take some work, but Apollo wasn't afraid of hard work. Before he could do anything about Set, though, he had to take care of Apophis.

"I promise I'll be careful," he said as he leaned closer and kissed Set's cheek.

Set narrowed his eyes, but he didn't tell Apollo to fuck off. Instead, he nodded, then turned toward the house.

Apollo wasn't worried. Whatever happened, Set would have his back.


Set watched the house. He didn't know where Apollo had gone when he'd attacked Apophis, but he wasn't surprised to see that this place was luxurious. It was big and had several cars parked in front of it, and Set could see a pool behind the house.

The place was eerily silent, which made him worry. He had no way to know if Apophis was here, and he had no clue what they'd do if he was. Leave, probably. Apollo had already tried to fight Apophis, and that hadn't ended well. They couldn't rush into it. They needed to take the plan step-by-step, and the first step was to defeat Maahes.

"Ready when you are," Apollo said.

"As long as you can keep your mouth shut, we can go now."

Apollo grinned. "I don't like keeping my mouth shut, but I'll make an exception for you. We'll talk once this is over."

It sounded like a threat, and it probably was. Set knew what Apollo wanted to talk about, and he wasn't ready. He hadn't admitted many things, even to himself, and he didn't know if he could admit them to Apollo. He doubted Apollo would let it go, though. It wasn't his style.

His eyes widened when Apollo strode toward the house. He'd thought they'd teleport in or maybe sneak in through a window, not that they'd knock on the door. He rushed after the Greek god, but it was too late. Apollo had already knocked.

The door opened, and Apollo stared at the young woman on the other side of it. She was only wearing a bikini, and she was visibly shaking. Set didn't think she was scared of Apollo. He smiled that smile of his that made everyone like him, and she relaxed until a noise came from behind her. She jumped and looked over her shoulder, but no one appeared.

"We're looking for a god," Apollo said.

The woman licked her lips. She wore makeup and her hair was done. She was lovely, all blonde hair and tanned skin, but she was uneasy.

"A god with only one hand?" she asked.

Apollo beamed at her. "Exactly. Is he here?"

"He's in the back." She hesitated. "Are you going to take him away?"

"We will, but he won't come willingly. Go upstairs, and don't come out for a while."

She nodded and left them by the open door. She didn't even tell them to come in. She just rushed for the stairs, grabbing another woman who was coming down them and pulling her back upstairs. This woman, too, wore only a swimsuit, which made Set wonder what this place was. Maybe they were roommates.

He and Apollo walked in and closed the door. As silent as the house was, they could hear voices in the direction the woman had indicated now that they were in, so they headed that way. The place wasn't just luxurious. It was garish, with bright colors that hurt Set's eyes. He didn't understand how anyone could live there, but he quickly realized that no one actually lived in this house when he and Apollo stepped into the living room.

Maahes was sitting on a couch, surrounded by women who looked terrified. Anyone would be terrified of the two demons standing behind the couch, guarding Maahes while he kissed one of the women.

Set swore when the demons surged forward. They should have known Maahes wouldn't be alone after Apollo had attacked him and Apophis.

Apollo thrust a hand forward, and his sword appeared. It was so bright that it made Set squint, but he didn't have time to be in awe of Apollo and what he could do. He pushed his power into his hands, then used it to create two black swords just in time to cut down one of the demons when it reached him.

The first strike wasn't enough to kill the demon, but Set didn't waste time. He arched his swords toward the demon, cutting its head off.

The body slumped, and the women screamed. Set turned to them, scowling because he disliked this kind of noise. "Leave!" he ordered.

He was afraid Maahes would grab one of the women and use her as a shield, but he was scrambling to his feet, holding his jeans with one hand and waving his other arm around. Apollo was done with the other demon, and he reached Maahes first. Maahes had to let go of his jeans to get his weapon, which appeared as soon as his hand was free. His jeans slid down his legs, exposing him.

Set grimaced. They were at war, so what the fuck had Maahes thought, coming to what had to be a brothel? He'd been caught with his pants down—literally.

Apollo laughed and stepped aside to let one of the women rush past him. He raised his sword to Maahes's chin, and Maahes froze.

"Not so strong when you're caught by surprise, are you?" Apollo asked.

Maahes didn't answer. He glared at Apollo as if it would be enough to kill him.

Set had no doubt that Apollo was stronger. The only reason Maahes had managed to stab him the other day was that he'd taken Apollo by surprise and had attacked him from behind. Apollo had been fighting Apophis, so he'd been focused on him. No one would attack him from behind today, though.

Set would make sure of that.

"Drop it," Apollo ordered.

Maahes bared his teeth. "Why would I do that?"

"Because I won't ask as nicely the next time I have to."

Apollo batted Maahes's sword with his own. It clattered on the floor. Maahes looked at it for a second before turning his attention back to Apollo. He looked ridiculous with his dick hanging out, and it took a lot not to laugh in his face.

Set realized he didn't *have* to stop himself from laughing.

He didn't care about Maahes. The god would die soon, and since Set doubted he'd give them the answers they needed willingly, he'd be tortured first. This was nothing next to what awaited him.

"Pull up your jeans," Apollo ordered. "You're taking a little trip."

"I'm not coming with you," Maahes snarled.

Apollo lowered his sword toward Maahes's groin. "Are you sure?"

Maahes swallowed and carefully leaned down to pull up his jeans. Set couldn't look away from Apollo. Usually he was smiling and laughing, bouncing with energy, but not now.

Set had never seen him like this. There was a dark energy to him that told both Set and Maahes that he wouldn't hesitate to follow through with his threat. If Maahes made a wrong move, Apollo would cut him down. Apollo might be the god of the sun, and he might be a warm and good person, but he was also a powerful god. This wasn't the first time he'd had to deal with a situation like this one, and he withstood it with an intensity that made Set wonder if he'd be the same way in bed.

"I won't tell you anything," Maahes said once he was dressed.

Apollo rolled his eyes. "Sure you won't. You think you'll just have to deal with me, but you're wrong. I might be a good fighter, but I don't know what I'm doing when it comes to torture. Set, on the other hand, is the god of violence. I'm sure he won't have any problems getting answers out of you."

Maahes turned to Set, who grinned at him. It wasn't a nice smile, and he saw Maahes hesitate.

*Good.* Maahes *should* be afraid. Set had no problem being the god of violence. It was the way he'd been born, and it would never change. Sometimes violence was necessary, no matter what most people thought.

In this case, it definitely was.

They would get answers out of Maahes, including, hopefully, the name of the spy. Once they did, he would kill Maahes, eliminating the minor god from existence. No one would remember him except for what he'd done with Apophis, and that was how it should be.

Maahes didn't deserve to be remembered as anything but a coward and a traitor. He'd chosen his side, and he'd chosen wrong, because in the end, Ra would defeat Apophis.

Set didn't hesitate to put away his swords and reach for Maahes. If the minor god tried anything, Apollo would cut him down. Maahes snarled and tried to pull away, but Set gave him a good shake. He didn't look back at Apollo. He didn't need to. They both knew exactly where they were going.

They appeared in front of Nu's suite. Nu had offered their space for them to do this, and everyone had agreed it was a good idea. No one would dare enter Nu's suite if they weren't invited, and they had more than enough space not to have to use this one after this was over. Apollo found it funny that the Egyptian pantheon didn't have a dedicated area for this, but maybe they weren't as bloodthirsty as his pantheon.

He wasn't too sure about that when he looked at Set and found him pushing Maahes toward the door. Set wasn't bloodthirsty per se, but right now, he was angry and wanted answers. He'd do whatever he had to in order to get them, and he wouldn't hesitate. Some people might have disliked that, but not Apollo.

They were at war. They couldn't be delicate about anything, especially not now that they'd gotten their hands on Maahes.

Apollo snorted at his thoughts, earning himself a glance

from Set. So he beamed at Set, who rolled his eyes and opened the door.

Nu was sitting in the living area but got to their feet as soon as they walked in. Their gaze focused on Maahes, who cringed slightly. No matter how callous the minor god was, Nu was his grandparent. He might not have cared if Nu had been anything like, say, Zeus, but they weren't. They were good, and it was clear Maahes knew he'd disappointed them.

"You know where to go," Nu said, seemingly not caring one bit about what was about to happen. "Try not to get blood on my floor."

"I can't promise that," Set drawled.

"As long as you clean up afterward, I don't care. I'm going to get Ra."

They probably didn't want to listen to the screaming, and while Apollo would go with them normally, he wouldn't leave Set alone with Maahes. He doubted Maahes could do anything against Set, but he was still angry at the minor god for stabbing him in the back.

Set dragged a reluctant Maahes toward the back of the suite. Apollo had never been here, having only visited the living area, but Set seemed to know where he was going. They stepped out of the suite and crossed the yard, but they didn't stop there. They continued walking until they reached a small building hidden by trees and flowers. There was a fountain next to it, and the place looked too peaceful for what was about to happen.

Apollo swallowed. He knew how to defend himself and how to fight, and he never hesitated to take a life when he had to, but this was different. He'd never tortured anyone. He didn't know what Set would do exactly, but it made his stomach churn just to think of it. He wasn't angry or disgusted by Set for having to do it, but he wasn't sure how he'd take it.

Set opened the door of the small building and pushed

Maahes inside. Apollo followed, looking around. The building was a single empty room. He suspected there had been
furniture here before, but it was all gone except for one chair
placed at the center of the room. It faced the opening in the
wall that gave onto the yard. There were no windows, but Nu
didn't need windows when the weather was always perfect
at the palace. Apollo could feel the breeze on his skin, but instead of being pleasant, it made him shiver.

Set tied Maahes to the chair before turning to Apollo.
Apollo tried to smile, hoping Set wouldn't see how uncomfortable this made him. He should have known better. Set always saw everything, especially when it came to Apollo.

He came closer, and both of them stood behind Maahes.
"You should go," Set murmured.

Apollo shook his head. "I'm not leaving you, and I deserve
to see what you'll do to him after he stabbed me."

"You might deserve it, but you don't need to watch. You
know what's going to happen. I'll get the answers we need
and revenge for what he did to you."

"I'm not weak. I can stand here and watch you work."

Apollo was stunned when Set grabbed his arm and pulled
him closer. Their lips were suddenly touching, and it took
Apollo a second to realize that Set was kissing him. Since he
didn't know if this was the only time Set would kiss him, he
took advantage of it and pressed closer. Set made a pleased
sound and dug his fingers into Apollo's hair. He pushed his
tongue into Apollo's mouth, and Apollo groaned in pleasure.

The kiss didn't last nearly as long as Apollo wanted it to.
Seconds later, Set stepped away, leaving Apollo flushed and
wanting more. Apollo wanted to do so many things to Set, but
it probably wasn't a good idea to do it in front of a minor god
they were about to torture.

"Go outside," Set murmured. "I'll take care of this and join
you as soon as I'm done. You have nothing to prove to me and

no reason to stay here and watch. I know you're not weak, Apollo. You're one of the strongest men I've ever known, and not wanting to watch as I torture someone isn't going to change that. It's not going to change the way I feel about you."

Apollo's mouth was dry. "How do you feel about me?" he croaked.

Set kissed Apollo again, but this kiss was even shorter. He stepped away, his gaze never leaving Apollo's. "We'll talk about it once this is over."

Apollo was glad to be offered an out. He didn't actually *want* to stay and watch Set torture Maahes. He wanted to stay by Set's side to show him that he could do it and that he was worthy of being with him, but it looked like he didn't have to do it. Set already believed Apollo was worthy of being with him.

He swallowed and turned. He had no idea what Set would do, and he didn't want to find out. He'd expected to have to be stoic and wait until all of this was over to go outside and throw up in the bushes, but he'd rather not throw up at all, and this was what Set was offering.

How was Apollo supposed to not fall for him?

Set waited until Apollo had closed the door behind himself to turn to Maahes. The minor god was trying to get out of the chair, but Set had tied him too well. Maahes's arms were on the armrests, exposing his hand and the fact that he was missing one. He was starting to sweat as he pulled on his arms, but he wasn't going anywhere.

Not until Set was done with him.

Set slowly walked around him. He took off his suit jacket and rolled up the sleeves of his shirt, never once looking at Maahes. He could feel the minor god getting more agitated as the seconds ticked by, and he loved it.

The door opened before he could do anything. He looked up, ready to tell Apollo to leave, but it wasn't him. "What are you doing here?" he asked Nu.

"I want to know what he has to say."

"I can let you know once this is over. You don't have to stay and watch."

They stared at Set for a moment. Like always, Set felt they could see right into his heart. Maybe they could. They had powers most gods could only imagine. They were the reason the Egyptian gods existed.

"I won't think badly of you because of what you're about to do," Nu said. "I know who and what you are. You're my grandson, and nothing about this will push me away from you."

Set didn't know what to do. He couldn't force them to leave, and he wanted to believe them. They knew he was the god of violence and what that entailed. They wouldn't shy away from any of this.

He turned back to Maahes. "You can give us the answers we're seeking, or you can hurt."

Maahes snarled. "You'll have to kill me."

Set smiled at him. "I don't think that will be a problem."

Torture wasn't something he often did, but he didn't hate it. They needed answers, and this was who he was. Violence ran in his blood and his soul. He wouldn't stop sleeping because of what he was about to do. He wouldn't feel remorse. He'd just do his job and get Ra what he needed.

He raised a hand, thinking about where he should start. It would be better to start small and see how Maahes reacted. Set might not have to make too much of a mess, depending on how Maahes took torture.

He chose to create a small knife and stepped closer.

Maahes was a liar. He'd told Set that he'd have to kill him

and that he wouldn't get answers, but things didn't get that far. Maahes was a bloody mess by the time he finally broke down and told Set who the spy was and where all the remaining demons were located. Apophis was using them as guards and to attack humans, but he didn't have that many left. The humans had killed many of them while defending themselves and their countries, and while the humans had always lost the fight in the end, they'd done a good job.

Set stepped away from Maahes. He cleaned his hands with a rag, taking his time. He was afraid to look at Nu, who hadn't moved or said anything the entire time. They were still in the corner, watching Maahes.

"This will break Ra," they murmured.

Set sighed. He knew it would. No one wanted to hear their daughter was working with Apophis, but it was what Ra would have to live through. Thankfully, Frey would be by his side, but Set didn't imagine that it would be easy anyway.

Nu straightened their back. "But he has to know. We all do."

"We know what we're working with now. I'm not saying it will be easy to defeat Apophis, but it will be easier."

"And that's what we were seeking."

They continued staring at Maahes. Set wondered what they were thinking. Did they want to help him? After all, he was their grandchild.

But instead of going to Maahes, Nu put a hand on Set's shoulder. He looked down at them, afraid of what he was about to see in their expression, but they smiled, and everything was all right.

"Go wash up. Your man is waiting for you outside."

"He's not my man," Set grumbled.

"I don't think he'd agree with that."

"That's because he's an idiot."

Nu cupped Set's cheek. "He might be an idiot, but he's an

idiot who makes you smile. You've needed that for a long time."

Set didn't know what to say, so he nodded. He was sure now that Nu could see in his heart. They knew what he needed and what he yearned for.

They knew he felt like he'd found both of those things in Apollo.

It was terrifying. Set never trusted anyone, not even his own family. That had somewhat changed recently, but Apollo belonged to another pantheon. He was the opposite of everything Set was. They shouldn't work as a couple, but Set knew that if he welcomed Apollo into his life, they would. If Apollo had even one chance with him, he wouldn't let it go, and Set was tired. He didn't want to continue resisting when there was nothing he wished for more than being in Apollo's arms.

But he didn't know how to deal with feelings. He wasn't even sure he knew how to *have* feelings. Right now, they all had more important things to focus on, and that was what Set needed to prioritize.

He kissed Nu's cheek and stepped out of the building. Two guards stood by the door, and he ordered them to go inside as soon as Nu was done. Set had no idea what they were doing or saying to Maahes, and it wasn't his business.

Like Nu had said, Apollo was waiting outside. He was sitting on a bench, earbuds in his ears as he bobbed his head to the sound of whatever music he was listening to. Set took a moment to watch him. He still didn't understand what this golden god wanted with him and why he was so focused on him, but by now, he knew that nothing he could do or say would push Apollo away. Apollo didn't take no for an answer, especially not when it came to Set.

Apollo got to his feet and scrambled to get his earbuds out as soon as he saw Set. Set hadn't noticed that Ra and Frey were there, too, sitting on another bench. They both got up, too, and for a moment, Set hesitated.

He had to tell Ra about this, but he didn't want to hurt him. It was odd to feel this way when he and Ra were supposed to be enemies. They were the opposite of each other.

But so were Set and Apollo, yet in some strange way, they were perfect together.

Set swallowed and moved toward Ra. Ra's expression was grim, and Frey leaned against him, offering him the silent support he'd need soon. Thankfully, Apollo didn't ask Set how things had gone. For once, he was silent as he joined Set.

"You have the name of the spy?" Ra asked.

"I do."

Ra sucked in a breath and briefly closed his eyes. "I'm not going to like it, am I?"

"I'm really sorry, but no."

"I wasn't going to like it, whoever it was. I hate that someone from our pantheon, who knows what Apophis can and did do, betrayed us like that."

Set hated it as much as Ra. He didn't understand why anyone would want to ally with Apophis, but he didn't have to understand. It was what the spy had done and should be punished for.

# CHAPTER SIX

A pollo was annoyed. He wanted to focus on seducing Set after the kisses they'd shared, but he couldn't, because they had to catch the fucking spy. That meant he'd have to wait to get into Set's pants, and he disliked that.

He'd finally broken through Set's armored shell. Set was letting him in, and Apollo didn't want to let anyone ruin that, especially not the spy.

He looked around Nu's living room. Would people attending the meeting notice if he dragged Set out? For a moment, he tried to convince himself that no one would, but he realized Barnaby and Lance were staring at him. They were on the other side of the room, but when he caught them staring, they quickly rushed to his side. They sat next to him, and Barnaby leaned in.

"You know who the spy is?"

Apollo pouted. "Do we really have to talk about that? The spy bores me."

Lance blinked. "The spy *bores* you? They betrayed us and could have gotten all of us killed, and they bore you?"

"Set kissed me."

Both Lance and Barnaby stared. Apollo felt smug that they were so shocked, although he wondered if he should be. Hadn't they known this would happen? Had they thought that Set would continue resisting Apollo's charms? That he could *have* resisted them?

Lance patted Apollo's knee. "That's great. The two of you are together, then?"

Apollo groaned. "I don't know. He just kissed me and told me we'd talk later, but we haven't talked yet, and now I'm overthinking this. If he kissed me, it's because he wanted to, right? Because he wants me?"

"I'm sure he does."

"But if you're not sure, we could come up with a plan to help you with that," Barnaby offered. "I mean, now probably isn't the best moment to do this, but I'm sure Set will need time to rest. You could help distract him."

"I can do that. I don't need a plan, though. My natural charm will take care of it."

Barnaby snorted. "Maybe you should remind your natural charm that Set wants to strangle you on a regular basis."

Apollo grinned. "But that's part of my natural charm."

"Just go for it," Lance said. "The next time the two of you are alone, kiss him and tell him you want him."

He made it sound so easy, and maybe it was. Things between Apollo and Set had been complicated since the beginning, but Apollo felt they were finally getting somewhere. Maybe they didn't have to be complicated anymore. Maybe talking to Set would be enough.

And if it wasn't, Apollo could just kiss Set again.

"Where is he, anyway?" Lance asked.

"He went back to Maahes."

They'd gotten the answers they needed yesterday, but Set had been convinced that Maahes could tell them more, so he'd insisted with Ra that they wait to do anything. He wanted more time alone with Maahes, which was what he was doing today. Apollo had stayed behind this time. He already knew what was happening, and he didn't need to be anywhere near it.

"Do you think we could go there?" Barnaby asked.

Apollo frowned. "Why would you want to do that?"

Barnaby shrugged. "I'm curious."

"As curious as you might be, that's not a place for you."

Barnaby frowned. "Because I'm human?"

"It has nothing to do with that. It's not a place for me, either, and I'm a god. It's just not something most people should see or deal with."

Barnaby slowly nodded. "But Set is there."

"You have to remember who he is. He's not a danger to you or anyone here, but he can be dangerous. Violence is in his nature, even though deep inside, he's a purring pussy cat."

Lance laughed. "That's not how I would describe him."

But it was how Apollo would describe Set. He didn't think Barnaby and Lance had ever been allowed to see how Set was in a private setting, but he had. He knew that Set enjoyed soft pajamas and that he hated socks. He knew that Set drank tea every evening after dinner to help him sleep better. He might be the god of violence, but there was a soft center to him that Apollo wanted to protect.

He also wanted more people to see it, because that way they'd finally realize that Set wasn't as dangerous as everyone thought, but that wasn't something he could do. If Set wanted people to know him better, he'd have to let them in.

"Gods are complicated," he said. "*People* are complicated, and gods are people, even though sometimes that's easy to forget. Set might be the god of violence, but that's not all he is. At the same time, I don't think this is something easy for humans to accept."

Barnaby shrugged. "I'm aware that some people don't deserve to live. I have no problems with Set killing Maahes if that's what he needs to do to protect everyone."

Apollo stared at him. He didn't know much about Barnaby and Lance, did he? He just knew they were nice and that they were dead, but he had no idea how they'd died. From the sound of it, Barnaby's end hadn't been easy.

But it also hadn't been the end. He was here now, and from what Apollo could see, he was happy. He was in love with an Egyptian god and had a bright future — as soon as Apophis was taken care of, anyway.

Apollo would never berate Set for what he was doing. He'd seen and done a lot over the thousands of years he'd been alive, and he understood that sometimes, death was the only path ahead. He'd need to make sure that Set knew he understood and that he wouldn't hold this against him. Set was doing what was necessary to keep humanity and the gods safe. The only people who might resent him for that were people who didn't know what they were talking about.

And if they tried to go anywhere near Set, Apollo would make sure they'd regret it.

Set stared at Maahes. After spending two days in Nu's back shed, the minor god was in bad shape. He slumped against the chair, his black hair covering part of his face. He'd bitten his lip so hard that it was bleeding, and the air smelled of sweat and copper.

He had no hands now. Set had taken the second one, and that had worked. He was pretty sure that Maahes had told him everything he knew about Apophis and his plans. Taking his second hand had been the straw that broke the camel's back, or in this case, Maahes's spirit. He was utterly broken. He was breathing hard, and he'd stopped trying to free himself. His detached hand was on the floor in front of him, but he was avoiding looking at it.

Set was tempted to push it closer so that he couldn't.

"I told you that you'd tell me everything," he said.

Maahes bared his teeth. "You're a monster."

Set smiled coldly. "You're right. I *am* a monster, but nowhere near as bad as Apophis. What did you think you were going to get, allying with him? Power? Wealth? You're a god, for fuck's sake."

"I'm a minor god," Maahes snapped, lunging forward. He was still tied up, so he didn't get far. He growled and pulled on the ties that held his arms to the chair.

"I'm aware of that."

"No, you're not. You don't know what it's like to be a minor god, a god no one remembers and cares about. Not even my own pantheon remembered I existed until I allied with Apophis. He's the only one who did, and I don't regret giving him what he needed."

Set frowned. Maahes was right when he said that Set wasn't a minor god and couldn't understand what that was like, but he knew minor gods. He just had to look at his allies, like Qebui and Sed. Qebui was the god of the North wind, for fuck's sake. Who cared about the North wind?

The two of them were *very* minor, but they'd never had a problem with that. They'd helped when they could, and they'd chosen the right side. Major gods like Set and Ra had noticed them because they were helpful and wanted to do the right thing.

And here was Maahes, having lost both of his hands and soon his life because he'd chosen the wrong side. No one would have cared that he was a minor god if he'd been allied with them, and they would have tried to save him if he needed help. What would Apophis do? Even if he did notice that Maahes was missing, he wouldn't come for him. He wouldn't want revenge for his ally. He couldn't care less about Maahes or anyone else. The only person Apophis cared about was Apophis.

Set opened his mouth to tell Maahes that, but in the blink of an eye, Maahes was on his feet. It took Set a few seconds to realize that, somehow, he'd gotten free of the ties.

Maahes threw himself at Set, and Set acted instinctively,

raising both of his hands together and making a sword appear in his hold. Maahes was rushing toward him, and he didn't have time to stop or even slow down. He threw himself onto the sword, and it moved through him like butter.

Maahes's eyes widened. He flailed his arms, spurting blood everywhere, before lowering them as if he wanted to grab the sword that was sticking out of his stomach. He didn't have fingers to grab onto anything, though.

Blood dribbled from his mouth as he stared at Set. Even though Maahes had done nothing but create trouble and hurt people, Set felt sorry for him. He'd wanted to be seen, and when the wrong god had given him attention, he'd fallen for it.

Set withdrew his sword from Maahes's body. Maahes dropped to the floor, rolling on his back. Blood spread under his chest, and Set briefly wondered if they'd be able to get all of it out of the floor.

He crouched next to Maahes. "I'll make it quick."

Maahes smiled. His teeth were red now. "Why would you do that?"

"Because I'm not as cruel as Apophis."

Maahes laughed. "You'll see how cruel he is soon. He'll kill all of you and avenge my death."

Set highly doubted that. Apophis *would* try to kill them, but it wouldn't be to avenge Maahes. No, no one would be avenging Maahes's death.

He got to his feet and swung his sword. There was one last gurgle, then silence.

Set sucked in a breath. His sword vanished, and he pressed his hands against his eyes. He was tired, but this still wasn't over. Before he could have his happily ever after — if he could ever have one, considering the god he was — they still had to defeat one major enemy.

Apophis.

They had more information about him and his plans now, but it still wouldn't be easy. The thought of what awaited them was scary, even to Set. He and Ra had defeated Apophis once before, and he was sure they could do it again, but there was a little voice at the back of his mind that wondered.

Things were different now. It wasn't only that thousands of years had passed and Apophis was probably stronger than he ever had been. It was also that Set had someone he cared about.

Apollo was right in the middle of this fight, and Set already knew it would be useless to try to convince him to go back to his pantheon. Apollo wouldn't stay out of the fight. When they faced Apophis, he'd stand right next to Set, and he'd fight alongside him. He might even die.

Set grunted. Things had been much easier when he didn't care about anyone. He didn't have to worry about them getting hurt or dying. Now, he had Apollo, but also the others. He didn't want anyone to get hurt, but that was impossible. They were about to fight Apophis, and they were bound to lose someone.

But who?

# CHAPTER SEVEN

Set stared at Ra. Ra looked heartbroken but steady, and Set had no doubt that he was telling himself that they were doing the right thing. They *were* doing the right thing.

But it couldn't be easy to do the right thing against one of his daughters.

Set had no idea what Tefnut was thinking or what she'd been thinking when she decided to turn to Apophis's aside. Maybe she'd felt like Maahes had—wanting someone to see him and recognize that even though he was a minor god, he had value. Maybe she was just selfish and cruel like Apophis, although Set had never seen her like that. Maybe Apophis had forced her into it, threatening her family and Ra.

Whatever the reason, she'd made the wrong choice. She'd chosen Apophis, and she was about to pay for it.

Ra shook his head. "I still don't understand why."

Frey leaned against him, and Ra wrapped an arm around his shoulders. They supported each other in a way that made Set wonder if he and Apollo could have the same. They'd kissed a few times, and they were closer than Set had ever been to anyone else, but it still felt fragile. They hadn't talked about it, and while Set knew what Apollo wanted since Apollo wasn't shy about his needs and wants, that didn't mean it would work.

He wasn't even sure what he wanted beyond being with Apollo. It was odd to feel that way, though. It didn't feel like him, and he couldn't help but wonder if it *was* him. What had happened to him that he suddenly wanted a relationship with a golden god like Apollo? Was it because with Apophis attacking them, there was a risk he wouldn't make it? Was this second fight reminding him that even though he was a god, he could die, and if he did, he'd lose everything?

"I don't think you can understand," Frey murmured. "She was probably scared that Apophis would kill her and everyone else. She might have wanted to protect herself and you. You could ask her, but I don't know if it's the best thing to do."

Ra rubbed a hand over his face. "The why doesn't matter. She knew she was doing the wrong thing, but she still did it."

Set agreed, but it was much easier for him. He and Tefnut were related—she was Set's grandmother—but he couldn't even remember the last time he'd talked to her. He wasn't sure he ever had.

But she was Ra's daughter. That meant something to Ra, more than it meant to Set. Set couldn't say he'd be happy with what they would do, but he wouldn't be heartbroken like Ra.

Family was complicated, especially when it was a godly family. They were messy, to say the least.

"We should feed her false information," Set said.

Both Ra and Frey looked up at him. Frey nodded, but Ra just stared.

Set leaned forward on the couch and tapped his fingertips on the coffee table. "We can make sure she finds out where you'll be on a given date. If she knows you'll be alone, she might try to attack you. She might also tell Apophis where you'll be, and he'll come for you."

"Then he can't go alone," Frey said.

"I wasn't planning on letting him go alone. I'll be there with him, of course." Family hadn't mattered much to Set before, but things had changed. Ra was his great-grandfather. Beyond that, he was a good person, and he was trying to do the right thing. He wanted to save humanity, which was the same thing Set wanted.

Hopefully, they'd manage to do so.

"We have to be careful how we feed her that information," Ra said. "We can't just go up to her and tell her. If we're not careful, she'll know something's wrong."

"We need someone close to us who could've easily been told about this but who wouldn't think much about talking in front of others even though it's supposed to be a secret. Someone who talks a lot, maybe."

Frey arched a brow. "Apollo sounds perfect."

He was right. Apollo was close to Set, and through him, to Ra. He was a known charmer, and he talked a lot. He would never spread important secrets, but only the people who knew him best were aware of that. A lot of others, like Set had in the beginning, believed he was airheaded and that he only thought about himself. That couldn't be further from the truth, but Tefnut didn't know that. If Apollo babbled about Ra needing time alone and where he'd be, she'd probably think he was an idiot and run to Apophis with the info.

It was a good plan. Set disliked the thought of putting Apollo in danger, but as long as he limited himself to playing such a small part in the trap, things would be fine.

The problem was that Apollo was stubborn and was planning to be involved. He was strong and powerful, and he could make the difference they needed, but he might get hurt, and that wasn't something Set was willing to consider.

Unfortunately, he would have to. Apollo wouldn't stay back just because Set asked him to.

Set sighed. "I'll talk to him. I don't think it'll be a problem, though. He'll be happy to be involved."

"*You* don't look happy," Frey said.

Set snorted. "Are any of us? I want this to be over. I want Apophis destroyed once and for all so we can all forget about him and focus on living our lives."

Before, it wouldn't have been very different from the life Set had for the past hundreds of years. Now, though, he had a chance at something important with Apollo, and he wouldn't allow anyone to ruin that.

Not himself, and definitely not Apophis.


Apollo was bored. That happened often, but usually he could find things to distract himself. He could go to the human realm, have fun with someone, or maybe do something like surfing. He missed the ocean, dammit, and it was all Apophis's fault.

He rolled onto his back and stared at the ceiling of his bedroom. He was comfortable here, although he'd be even more comfortable in Set's bed. He was tempted to go there and deal with whatever Set had to say about it afterward, but he didn't want to push things too hard. Set had finally broken down the other day when he'd kissed Apollo, but they'd barely seen each other since then, and Apollo still didn't know what it had meant.

Had Set kissed Apollo to convince him to leave? Maybe he'd just wanted to distract him and had decided that would be the best way to do so. He wouldn't have been wrong. The kiss had effectively distracted Apollo, and he'd been thinking of nothing else since it had happened.

But maybe Set had *wanted* to kiss Apollo. Maybe he was finally over whatever crap he'd been telling himself as an excuse to stay away and had decided to give their relationship a chance. It was what Apollo had wanted from the beginning, and he hated that he didn't know what was going on. The best way to find out would be to ask Set, but how was he supposed to do that when his man spent all of his time torturing Maahes and talking to Ra?

The sound of a door opening in the distance made Apollo

jump. For a moment, he listened, wondering who it was. It was early for Set to be home. He was the only one who would dare walk into these rooms, though, apart from Apollo. All the other gods seemed terrified of Set and of what he might do if he found them in his home, and they weren't wrong to feel that way. Set loved his privacy, and Apollo couldn't blame him for that.

He sat up as the sound of footsteps came closer. His bedroom door was open, but Set still knocked as he peeked in.

Apollo beamed at him, suddenly pleased the only thing he'd put on this morning was his tiny pair of shorts. Set had already been gone when Apollo had woken up, so he hadn't seen them.

Apollo wiggled to the edge of the mattress, his smile widening when Set's gaze caught on his body.

Apollo looked good. He was a god, so he could decide what aspect he had. He'd always gone with blond curls and kept his body trim and lightly muscled.

From the appreciation in Set's gaze, it looked like it was the right decision.

Set cleared his throat. "Can I come in?"

"Always. You don't have to ask."

"I have to talk to you."

Apollo frowned. That didn't sound good. When someone in a relationship said they needed to talk to the other, it usually ended in a breakup. "Are you going to break up with me?" he asked.

Set stepped into the room. "We'd have to be together for me to break up with you," he pointed out.

Apollo pressed a hand over his heart as he sat up. "Are you saying we're not together?"

Set rolled his eyes. "We haven't talked about it, so I don't know what we are. That's not why I'm here, though. I wanted to talk to you about the spy and a plan that Ra, Frey, and I have come up with. It involves you, and while you're allowed to say no, we think you're the best god for the job."

Apollo hadn't expected that. It wasn't as good as Set declaring his undying love for him, but it was close. These people finally needed him, and he couldn't wait to help.

He bounced on the mattress. "Tell me."

Set looked around the room. Apollo wondered what he was looking for, but he didn't have to wonder for long. Set dragged a chair closer to the bed, and after dumping the clothes that had been draped on it onto the mattress, he sat down and leaned forward. "We want to feed the spy false information. We want her to think that Ra will be in a certain place at a certain time on his own. He'll be vulnerable, and hopefully, she'll take the chance to confront him or tell Apophis about it."

"What am I supposed to do in this scenario?"

"We think she won't believe what we say if we're the ones to tell her. We wouldn't announce something like that during a meeting because we know there's a spy, and we know better than to talk about it where others can hear us."

"But I'm an idiot who talks too much."

To Apollo's surprise, Set leaned forward and squeezed his knee. He didn't remove his hand, and Apollo stared at it for a moment. Set was touching him willingly. He was touching Apollo's bare skin with his, and he wasn't snarling or telling Apollo this meant nothing.

"You're not an idiot," Set said. "No one who matters thinks that you are, and while I don't like that people see you that way, it would come in handy in this case. I don't know why Tefnut is doing this, but she doesn't know you, so she would probably believe that you could spill that kind of information without worrying too much about it. She probably thinks that you don't really care about us, anyway. You belong to another pantheon, and while you're helping us now, it doesn't mean you care about us. You want to save humanity, but probably not our pantheon."

"Of course I want to save your pantheon."

Set smiled. "I know you do, but she doesn't. Most gods barely care about the gods in their own pantheon, let alone other pantheons."

Apollo didn't care that people thought he was an idiot. He knew that sometimes he behaved like one, but he didn't understand why gods were supposed to be stuffy and snobbish. He loved humans. They were creative and intelligent, and he didn't want humanity to be destroyed just because a god was pitching a fit.

He pressed his hand on top of Set's. "I'll help you. You don't have to try to convince me. I do have one condition, though."

Set frowned and leaned back. "Maybe I should ask someone else, then."

He wasn't going to get out of this that easily. "Or maybe you should listen to me." Apollo surged forward and kissed Set. It was quick, but it was their third kiss, and Apollo enjoyed it thoroughly.

"What do you want?" Set asked as he looked away.

If Apollo was right, he could see a slight pink color on his cheeks. It was adorable. "I want another kiss."

"You just had one."

"I want a real kiss, like the one you gave me before torturing Maahes, but I want it to be longer."

Set stared at Apollo. "That's it? You want a kiss from me?"

"That's all I want," Apollo promised.

In reality, he wanted so much more, but he didn't want Set to feel forced to give it to him. If things were going to work between them, they'd have to move slowly. Set was pricklier than a porcupine, and while Apollo felt he was making good progress, one wrong step would be enough to ruin everything.

Set squared his jaw and nodded. "All right. I'll kiss you."

Apollo beamed. He felt so light that he might start to float. He puckered his lips, and Set once again rolled his eyes — something he tended to do a lot when he was with Apollo. To be fair, everyone seemed to do that a lot around him.

Set leaned forward and pressed their lips together. Apollo was pretty sure he'd intended to keep it as short as possible, but that wasn't what Apollo wanted.

He hooked his arms around Set's shoulders and pulled him close as he opened his mouth. Set made a surprised sound, but he came easily. He wrapped his arms around Apollo's waist and slipped his tongue into Apollo's mouth, making him groan.

*This* was what Apollo wanted. He needed to feel close to Set, and he was sure Set felt the same. It didn't matter how prickly he was. His insides were soft and squishy, and he had more feelings than he'd ever admit to.

Apollo tilted back, taking Set with him. He wasn't sure why Set didn't resist, but he took it as a win. He stroked his tongue against Set's, swallowing Set's whimper and feeling like Set had just handed him the world.

He made to wrap his legs around Set, but the movement must have startled Set. He jerked away and stared at Apollo with wide eyes as if he couldn't believe what they'd just done.

"You had your kiss," he said.

Apollo pouted. "I want another one."

"You only wanted one."

"I only *asked* for one, but I want every kiss you're willing to give me and so much more."

Set stared for a moment. "Do your job, and I'll give you more."

Apollo beamed and watched as Set scrambled off the bed and out the door. He was acting like a spooked animal, and in a way, he was. This had been a lot for him but not enough for Apollo.

Apollo flopped down onto his back and looked at the ceiling. He was beaming like an idiot, and he didn't care. This was going to work.

He was sure of it.


Set wasn't proud to say that he ran away from Apollo. He didn't know what else to do.

Apollo overwhelmed him in a way no one else ever had. Set didn't know what to do with him or how to react to what he did. Apollo demanded things no one else would have dared demand from Set, and he wasn't afraid of him.

Everyone was afraid of Set.

But not Apollo. Instead of being afraid, he looked at Set like he wanted to devour him. From his behavior and what he said, Set could see that he wanted a long-term relationship, and he didn't understand that. He didn't think he ever would, but he was done resisting.

That didn't mean that giving in was easy.

It was anything but. Set didn't *have* relationships. He fucked anyone he wanted, but that was where it ended. He rarely even saw the same person twice, and most of the time, people had sex with him because they thought it was exciting to be with the god of violence. Set didn't like that, but he also didn't care much what people thought of him.

But he cared what Apollo thought of him so very much.

Only Apollo had ever managed to make him feel unsteady and like he had no idea what he was doing. It was why he was running from his suite, not knowing where to go. He could go to the human realm, but that would be dangerous. On the other hand, he only ever stayed in his rooms when he was in the palace, and right now, he couldn't be there.

What did that leave him?

His feet took him in the direction of Nu's suite. Maybe it was because he'd spent a lot of time there lately, or maybe because his grandparent had never looked at him with fear or disgust like a lot of the other gods had. They knew what Set was and that he was needed just as much as Ra or any other god. He and Ra were part of the same balance—a balance Apophis was trying to break.

But Nu didn't care. They loved Set, even though they'd been there when Set had tortured Maahes the first time. They knew *exactly* who he was.

They still loved him.

He didn't even have to knock. The door swung open as soon as he reached it, and Nu looked up at him with a smile. "I got a call from Thoth. He said he saw you rushing down the hallway toward my rooms and thought I should be aware of it."

Set glared. "Since when do people care where I'm going?"

They stepped aside to let him in. "People always care about where you're going."

"Because they're afraid I'm going to attack them."

"Some of them." Nu closed the door. "But a lot of us just care about you. I can see that Thoth was right. You do look out of sorts."

Set sucked in a breath, and to his horror, when he opened his mouth, everything came out. "It's Apollo. We kissed several times, and I have no idea what to do with that or how to behave. I don't understand why, but he seems to want a relationship with me, and I have no idea how those work, especially not with a god like Apollo. Why does he want this with me? He's so good and sweet, and I'm the exact opposite. He shouldn't even look at me twice, yet he's been trying to worm his way into my life since we first met, and I don't think anything I can say will stop him. He knows what he wants, and for some reason, what he wants is *me*."

Set snapped his mouth shut and groaned. What the fuck was happening to him?

Nu chuckled. "That's a lot."

"I was fine before meeting him," Set said as he started pacing. "Everyone left me alone, and I loved it. I don't know anything about relationships. People don't usually care about me that way."

"Apollo doesn't care what kind of god you are, though."

"He doesn't seem to. He knows what I did to Maahes, but he's still here. He still wants me."

Set didn't understand why, but he was starting to realize that maybe he didn't have to. Apollo wanted him, even knowing who Set was and what he did. He might be a little messy and airheaded sometimes, but he was an intelligent person. If Set was so horrible, Apollo wouldn't want him, right?

Set had spent so much time keeping other people away because they were scared of him and he hated the way they looked at him that he hadn't thought that maybe not *everyone* was afraid of him. Most of his family didn't seem to be, and Apollo definitely wasn't. Hell, even Barnaby and Lance were comfortable with Set, and they were human.

Maybe Set wasn't so unlovable after all.

"That's good," Nu said as they patted Set's arm. "I've been watching you for a while now, and I disliked how lonely you were."

"I'm not lonely," Set said with a scoff.

Nu didn't look like they believed him. "Fine. I hated how alone you were and how far away you kept people, and I'm glad Apollo managed to break through that. You don't have to be with him if he's not the kind of person you want, but I think it would do you good. He might not belong to our pantheon, but he balances you, and that's what you need. It's what we all need."

Maybe Nu was right. Set hoped they were, because he couldn't see himself without Apollo anymore. As annoying as the other god was, he'd pushed his way into Set's life and into his heart, and with how stubborn he was, there was no way Set would ever be able to kick him out. He was pretty sure that Apollo had fully moved into his suite by now, and if he hadn't, it wouldn't be long.

Apollo had found a home with Set, even though Set had been resisting and pushing him away. Maybe Set could do the same. Maybe he could find a home with Apollo.

# CHAPTER EIGHT

A pollo was ready to play his most important role. He looked around, slightly unsettled at the thought that the spy was in the room with him and the others. It was hard to believe that one of the people who'd promised to fight Apophis was working for him instead.

Apollo couldn't help but look for her, but he couldn't see her. She was in the room, though. Set had confirmed it when Apollo had looked his way. Now, Apollo needed to do his part.

He cracked his knuckles and tilted his head to the right, then to the left. When he felt ready, he looked down to see that Barnaby was staring at him.

"You look like you're ready to start a fight," Barnaby said.

Apollo grinned. "If I were, I'd win it."

Barnaby shook his head, but he was smiling. "There's no need for you to start any kind of fight."

Because they both knew the biggest fight for them was looming on the horizon.

Apollo plastered a smile on his lips and tried to focus on his job. "I don't know. Fighting with Set isn't that bad." They weren't real fights, anyway.

"I bet the makeup sex is great."

Lance, who was never far from Barnaby, elbowed him. "You can't say that."

"Why not? Aren't you the least bit curious about how Set is in bed?"

Apollo wished he knew. "I wouldn't tell you even if I

knew."

Lance and Barnaby stared. "You mean you don't know what he's like in bed?" Barnaby asked. "I thought for sure the two of you were fucking."

"Not for lack of trying on my part, but Set's very focused on the fight ahead. He's been dealing with Maahes, and that's taken a while." Apollo looked around, then leaned forward. "Plus, he and Ra are planning something."

Lance looked worried, but Barnaby's eyes sparkled as he leaned closer, too. Apollo felt a bit guilty at the thought of using these two, and he hoped they wouldn't be angry at him when they found out. He could talk to someone else, maybe one of the gods, but he felt closer to the humans. He would even consider them friends, which wasn't something he'd expected when he'd decided to get involved in this fight.

"Can you tell us what they're planning?" Barnaby asked.

"He shouldn't," Lance hissed. "We know there's a spy."

Apollo winked at him. "I doubt the spy is listening in. Besides, after Maahes, I wouldn't be surprised if they weren't here at all."

Barnaby frowned, but Lance's focus was on Apollo. After a few seconds, his eyes widened, and Apollo winked.

"Besides, it's not that much of a secret," he explained. "Ra came to me to ask for advice since both of us are sun gods. He wanted to know if my pantheon had anything that would help him be stronger, so I told him about this temple where a lot of the gods in my pantheon go before a fight. I've never been because I don't need that kind of boost, but I've heard that it helps focus power. I don't know if it'll be useful, but Ra needs all the help he can get."

It was a lie. Nothing like that existed, and as far as Apollo knew, nothing could make a god more powerful. They'd needed a reason for Ra to be hanging out alone, and this worked as well as anything else would have.

"When is he going?" Lance asked.

Apollo was pretty sure Lance understood what Apollo was doing. He didn't know if Barnaby did, but that didn't matter. Apollo just needed to talk.

He was speaking loudly enough that he knew the spy would hear him, but not so loud that it would be clear something was up. He hoped the spy would fall for it, but at the same time, it made him wonder.

If the spy did fall for it, she would tell Apophis. What if Apophis decided to take Ra out while he was alone? They were doing this in the hope of neutralizing the spy after getting rid of Maahes, but Apophis might decide this was too good an opportunity. Maybe he wouldn't want to waste it and would choose to attack Ra.

The problem was that Ra couldn't bring every ally he had along with him. He and Set would be going, but that was it. They couldn't afford to have the spy realize it was a trap, which meant most people would have to stay behind. Apollo disliked the fact that he wouldn't be there to watch Set's back, but he told himself that Set didn't need him. He'd survived until now, after all. He was a powerful god. Even if Apophis attacked, Set could defend himself and Ra. Besides, he and Ra had managed to trap Apophis before. It wouldn't be easy, but Apollo was sure they could do it a second time, even if they were on their own.

But maybe he should follow Set, just in case.

"Soon. He wants to be ready when the fight starts."

"Where's the temple?" Barnaby asked.

"Where else can it be but in Greece? Other gods aren't supposed to go there, but no one will notice, and I thought it would be for the best to use all the help we can get."

"That doesn't sound like a great idea. What if one of the Greek gods realizes what's happening and tries to kick Ra's ass?"

Apollo patted Barnaby's shoulder. "Ra will be fine. He knows to be discreet, and even though my father doesn't want anything to do with what's happening with Apophis, I'm sure the others realize that something needs to be done. They won't intervene. I doubt anyone will notice something's happening, anyway. The temple is almost completely destroyed, and only very few people know it's there. It's why there aren't any tourists around."

Apollo caught movement with the corner of his eye. He didn't turn to see who was skulking by, but he didn't have to. He was sure it was the spy.

He leaned even closer to Barnaby and Lance to give them more details about where the temple was and when Ra would be going. He could tell Tefnut was there, listening to them, so he focused on Barnaby and Lance instead.

Lance shook his head. "It feels like you shouldn't tell us all of this."

"It's fine. I trust you, and I know you won't tell anyone."

"I swear we won't," Barnaby said.

Lance kept glancing in the direction of the spy. Apollo didn't know if he was aware of who it was, but he needed to distract him before Tefnut realized something was up. To distract Lance, he swung an arm around Lance's shoulders and pulled him toward Set, who was on the other side of the room, talking to Ra. "Come on. I miss my boo."

Lance's cheeks flushed. "He's going to kill you if he hears you call him that."

"I can't wait for it to happen," Barnaby said gleefully.

They were effectively distracted. Apollo risked a glance behind them as they moved. Though he'd been told who the spy was, he wasn't sure he could recognize her, but he did. She was just another goddess and looked like she belonged in this room, but her gaze was shifty, almost as if she was trying to find a reason to leave.

Probably to tell Apophis what she'd just heard.

Apollo still wasn't a hundred percent comfortable with this plan, but he'd played his role. Hopefully, he wouldn't regret having a hand in this. They didn't know if Apophis himself would try to attack Ra, and while Apollo didn't think so, he still couldn't help but wonder what would happen if he did.

"Here's my boo," he exclaimed when they reached Set and Ra.

Ra looked amused, but Set's gaze was intense. He looked from Apollo to Lance and Barnaby, and Apollo could see the question he wasn't asking in his expression. He quickly nodded, then grinned wider. "Barnaby was wondering what you're like in bed. I had to tell him that, unfortunately, I don't know."

Barnaby spluttered and turned so red that Apollo laughed. "I promise that's not what I said," Barnaby quickly explained.

"Isn't it? I could have sworn that was what you were asking."

Barnaby elbowed Apollo in the ribs. Apollo loved that Barnaby and Lance didn't seem to care that he was a god and treated him like they did everyone else.

It made him feel like he was part of something, maybe even a family. It wasn't something he was used to. His family was a mess, and that hadn't changed over thousands of years. It probably never would.

But maybe it didn't matter because it looked like Apollo had found a better one.


Set was amused, but he didn't know how to behave. Why was Apollo talking about how Set was in bed when they hadn't gotten that far yet?

He looked down at the two humans. Barnaby looked like he wanted to run, and Set wondered if he was afraid of him.

He wouldn't be surprised. Set was the one who always projected the impression of being angry and not accepting people teasing him. He'd done so because he wanted to be left alone, but that had changed since Apollo had barged into his life.

A lot had changed since Apollo had decided that he and Set were supposed to be together. It was overwhelming, but Set was surprised to realize that he wouldn't have it any other way.

At least it looked like Apollo had managed to get the information that Ra would be alone in a temple in Greece to the spy. Set had noticed Tefnut hovering close to Apollo earlier, but he'd tried not to stare in case she realized what was happening. This was supposed to be a trap for her and maybe for Apophis. It wouldn't do any good if she understood something was up.

Apollo was still talking with Barnaby, who kept slapping his shoulder as if instead of a powerful god, he was one of Barnaby's friends. Lance kept looking from one to the other, clearly amused. They were all distracted, so Set leaned toward Ra. "I think she heard them," he murmured.

Ra was good at controlling his expression, which was a relief. Set knew how hurt he was by what was happening, and he understood. He wished he could take the pain away from his great-grandfather, but there was nothing anyone could do. Tefnut had made her choice.

Set tried to imagine what it would be like to find out that one of his children had betrayed him like this. He had four, but like with most gods, he wasn't close to them. Maybe it was time to change that, or at least it would be time to do so when this war was over. He wasn't sure what Apollo would think of him wanting to get to know his kids, but it was something to think about.

Ra nodded. "Good."

"I'm really sorry."

Ra shook his head. "Don't be. You had nothing to do with her decision, and like always, when I need you, you're standing by me, ready to help. I know you like your reputation of being a monster because it keeps people away, but you never were one."

The conversation was making Set uncomfortable. He'd tried so hard to keep everyone away for thousands of years that he didn't know what to do now that he couldn't anymore. He'd chosen his side, but even more, he'd opened up to people in a way he hadn't before. He might not have if Apollo hadn't barged into his life, but there was no getting out of this anymore.

Apollo was like a koala. He was clinging to Set, and Set was pretty sure he wouldn't let go unless he didn't have a choice.

It was a lot, especially for a god who'd been on his own for so long. Since Apollo was distracted with Barnaby and Lance, Set stepped away. They'd been having another meeting, which was why everyone was gathered today, but with nothing new to talk about, it had quickly devolved into what looked like a party. Small groups had formed, and people were talking about Apophis and what he was doing in the human realm. They were getting ready to fight him, and Set could almost see the tension in the room.

Everyone was afraid. The fact that they were gods didn't mean they couldn't be killed, and when it came to Apophis, there was a big chance they would be. Set didn't want to think about it because it would be useless, but others probably couldn't avoid doing so.

Tefnut was nowhere to be seen, and Set hoped it was because she was already planning her next move. She'd have to tell Apophis about this, but he probably wouldn't come out himself. Killing Ra was what Apophis was ultimately aiming for, but not like this. Not when he was alone visiting an isolated temple where no one in the human realm would see them.

What Apophis wanted more was glory. He wanted people to bow down to him and be afraid of him. If he was going to kill Ra, he'd do so in a very public way.

That didn't mean he wouldn't try to hurt Ra before then, though. He might ask his spy to prove herself to him, or he might send her ahead, not caring if Ra killed her. Apophis wasn't known for caring about people, not even about the people who worked for him. Tefnut would regret allying with him.

But it was too late to go back.

Set was relieved when he left the big room. The noise of the many voices softened instantly when the door closed behind him, and he sucked in a breath. He was sure Apollo would quickly notice he wasn't there anymore, which meant he couldn't go home. Instead, he decided to walk through the gardens. He needed some time alone, something Apollo wasn't eager to give him. It was almost as if he thought that Set would run if he wasn't in his sight.

Sometimes, that was tempting. Set had no idea how to deal with the many feelings Apollo created in him, but being alone for a while helped. By the time he returned to his rooms, he felt better. He didn't think he was ready to face Apollo, but he couldn't avoid it for much longer.

When he walked into his living area, he paused and listened. He couldn't hear anything, which was odd because he'd expected Apollo to be home by now. Had he stayed behind, maybe with Barnaby and Lance?

Whatever the case, Set was relieved. He moved toward the hallway that would lead him to his bedroom. As he walked past the couch, Apollo suddenly sat up, startling him. Set would never admit it, but he squeaked in surprise.

He scowled at Apollo. "What do you think you're doing?"

Apollo grinned.

Set didn't think there was ever a moment in which Apollo wasn't smiling, except maybe when he was sleeping.

"I was waiting for you."

"Hiding on the couch?"

"I wasn't hiding. I knew you'd try to avoid me, so I thought that making sure you couldn't see me would help."

"That's the definition of hiding."

Apollo shrugged. "Whatever. I might be hiding, but you're avoiding me."

Set suddenly felt the urgent need to go to his room. "I have things to do, Apollo."

"Sure. Go do them. But when this is over and you return from the temple, we'll talk."

Set disliked the feeling that he was running away, but that was what he was doing. He was running from Apollo.

He decided that the best way to keep the other god away was to shift. He didn't often do it, but the feelings would be less overwhelming if he was in his animal form. He would be able to hide better, too, which would come in handy when Apollo came to look for him.

Set only waited until his bedroom door was open to shift. His clothes shifted with him.

He wasn't a real animal like most of the other gods in his pantheon. His animal looked like some of the real ones, but not quite. He was some kind of dog, but once again, not quite a dog.

What he was didn't matter. He crawled under the bed, knowing it was ridiculous and that most people would laugh in his face if they ever found him in this position. Apollo probably would, too—but then he'd crawl under the bed with him. The more ridiculous something was, the more Apollo liked it.

Set slumped on the floor and curled into a tight ball. His tail brushed against his nose, and he buried his face against it.

He disliked feeling so unsettled, and it had come at the

worst possible moment. He was supposed to focus on Apophis and finding a way to defeat him once and for all, but instead, he could only think of Apollo and what he'd said just now.

They would talk once this thing with the temple was over. What did he want to talk about? Set could imagine all too well, and he wasn't looking forward to it. He liked Apollo, but he didn't know how to tell him that. He wasn't even sure he could. What if Apollo rejected him?

He softly snorted. Apollo wouldn't reject him. He'd already made his interest in Set clear, and he wouldn't back down.

Set wasn't sure how he felt about that.

# CHAPTER NINE

"This isn't what I expected," Set said as he looked around. "He did say the temple was in ruins," Ra said.

Apollo had said the temple was in ruins, but hardly more than a few stones still stood. Set wouldn't even have known it was a temple if Apollo hadn't told him about it. "Why should anyone believe you'd come here to become more powerful? There's nothing but ruins and plants here."

"A Greek god would know, but not Tefnut. She'll come."

Set winced. Either she would or Apophis would. Set wasn't looking forward to dealing with either of them, but it was necessary. Besides, it had gotten him out of talking with Apollo, which, as far as he was concerned, was a positive aspect.

Ra sighed. "You should go and hide. I'm sure she'll be here soon, and I'll need you when she arrives."

He didn't have to say anything else. Set wanted to tell him everything would be all right, but it would be a lie. Nothing would be all right for Ra until Apophis was dealt with.

Apollo had mentioned a space higher up in the mountain from which Set would be able to see what was happening under him. He'd be able to tell if Ra needed help, but no one would be able to see him even if they looked up.

Set made his way there, lost in his thoughts. It was the only reason he didn't see Apollo until he was basically on top of him.

When he reached Apollo, he swore and crouched next to him. "What are you doing here? Apophis could arrive at any moment."

Apollo smiled. He was golden and beautiful, so much so that it made Set's heart hurt. "I didn't want to let you face all of this on your own."

"This wasn't the plan. You're not supposed to be here."

"You might need help. What if Apophis comes?"

Set grabbed Apollo's shoulder and gave him a shake. "Then I don't want you here. You can't face Apophis again."

Apollo pouted. "Why not? He doesn't have his guard dog to stab me in the back anymore."

The sound of voices under them startled Set, and he realized he'd been so focused on Apollo that he hadn't paid attention to what Ra was doing.

He pulled Apollo closer and kissed him. It was hard, and their teeth clashed, but it made Apollo shut up, which was what Set was aiming for.

"If you keep your mouth shut, I'll kiss you again later," he murmured against Apollo's lips.

Apollo nodded quickly, and Set let go of him. He leaned forward to look at Ra, not at all surprised to see that Tefnut was standing in front of him.

Set glanced behind himself at Apollo, who looked like he didn't know what to do. "Go home. Ra and I will finish this."

Apollo nodded without arguing, which had to be a miracle. He vanished, and Set turned his attention back to Ra.

"What are you doing here?" Ra asked.

"I knew you would be alone," she answered.

"Why did you do it? Why ally with Apophis?"

Set winced. Ra was going straight to the point. Set wasn't surprised, because he knew Ra wanted answers, but there might have been better ways to get them.

"Because you're going to get all of us killed. Apophis has always been the strongest one. The only reason you defeated him before was that you had help."

"I have help this time around, too."

"It won't be enough this time. Apophis is stronger, and he's growing more powerful as time passes. If I hadn't allied with him, I would have been killed like all of you will be."

She'd admitted to everything. Set wished Ra would act on it. They'd already talked about what to do with her, and they'd agreed on a punishment.

Tefnut wouldn't be killed. Since she'd allied with Apophis, she would be punished like he'd been the first time he tried to destroy Ra. Osiris would lock her away in the darkness once she and Ra joined him and Thoth.

Ra wasn't giving anything away right now. He kept staring at his daughter, and while Set understood, he wanted to give Ra a good shake. This needed to be done, no matter who the spy was.

"You can still turn back from this," Ra said instead. "If you give me all the information you have on Apophis, I'll soften your punishment."

"I don't need you to soften anything. I knew what I was doing when I made my choice, and I don't regret it. I'm sorry, Father. I chose the winning side, and I won't change my mind." She straightened her back and looked around. "And soon Apophis will arrive, and we'll fight you. I'm not stupid enough to think I can take you by myself, but with him, I can do anything."

Set almost snorted. She really thought Apophis would come? He didn't care about anyone but himself, and he certainly wouldn't care about someone he manipulated and used as a spy.

For a few moments, everything was quiet. It was clear that Tefnut was waiting for Apophis to arrive, but like Set had guessed, he never did. She screeched and threw herself at Ra. Set scrambled to get to him. He shouldn't have worried, though. Ra was hurt by what his daughter had done, and he was too soft, but he wouldn't allow Tefnut to hurt him or his mission to defeat Apophis.

Ra caught Tefnut and twisted her around so that her back was against his chest. He immobilized her arms, and no matter how hard she tried to free herself, she was unable to. Ra stood strong, even though, from his expression, it was clear his heart was breaking.

Ra was whispering something to her, but Set doubted she was listening. She was still trying to get free, even though it was obvious she wouldn't be able to.

Set stepped forward. "I'll take her to the underworld."

Osiris knew what was happening, and he'd agreed to have them. He and Thoth were waiting in the underworld to lock her into the darkness. Frey would be there, too. Initially, he'd wanted to stand by Ra when he faced his daughter, but they'd decided it would be for the best if he stayed away. That was why he was with Osiris. He'd known Ra would need him, and since he hadn't been allowed to stay with him during the confrontation, he was waiting in the underworld. It was where Ra would need him the most.

"I'm coming," Ra said in an uncompromising tone.

"You don't have to."

He looked down at Tefnut. "I do."

Set wasn't going to argue. It would make this harder on Ra, but Ra knew what he was doing.

Set teleported to the underworld, but it took Ra a few more minutes to arrive. Set took advantage of the time to explain everything to Osiris, Frey, and Thoth. When Ra finally appeared with his daughter, the four of them wore identical grim expressions.

"I'm sorry it came to this," Thoth said.

Ra nodded at him. "Hopefully, it will give her enough time to realize what she did."

Tefnut was done screaming but not trying to fight her way out of Ra's embrace. Ra didn't even seem to realize it. He kept holding her as if she was precious, and to him, she was. She wasn't just a spy who'd given up many of their secrets to Apophis and who wouldn't have hesitated to stand by his side when he fought Ra. She was Ra's daughter, and she always would be.

It was hard to watch. Set knew that she wouldn't die and that nothing would happen to her while she was locked up in the darkness, but this meant she would vanish from their pantheon for hundreds of years, if not more. When she realized what was happening, she started screaming and begging her father to let her go. For a moment, Set thought that Ra might do it, but he stood strong, even though it was obviously breaking his heart.

Thankfully, Frey was there. He reached Ra as soon as Ra let go of his daughter. She tried to run, but she didn't get far. Thoth was weaving his magic, trapping her in a darkness that quickly grew.

Set closed his eyes. This was necessary, but his heart still broke a little. They would have to sustain a lot more losses in their fight against Apophis, which was hard to believe. There was a chance Set would lose someone he cared about, but he couldn't consider that option. He would have to be strong, just like Ra.

He wouldn't have a choice.


Apollo paced the length of the living room. He had faith in Set's abilities, but he was still nervous. How could he not be? There was a chance Set was fighting Apophis right now, and Apollo wasn't there to watch his back.

Hopefully, only the spy had gone to Ra. The problem was that Apophis wanted to get rid of Ra, and this would be the easiest way for him to do so. It was why they'd decided to try this. If Apophis thought he'd find Ra alone, he might be more inclined to attack, and Set could surprise him. He and Ra had defeated Apophis before, and Apollo kept telling himself that, but it didn't help.

They hadn't been alone when they defeated Apophis, but they were now. Apollo should have gone with Set, but Set had promised he'd be all right, and Apollo wanted to believe him. In a way, this was none of his business. He was a Greek god, not an Egyptian one, and Apophis belonged to the Egyptian pantheon. These gods knew Apophis better than Apollo ever could, and he needed to trust them when it came to what was happening.

He did trust them — both Set and Ra — but that didn't mean he wasn't worried or that nothing would happen to them.

There was also the fact that Set had been avoiding Apollo. Apollo wasn't offended. He understood that Set didn't know what to do with him or the feelings growing between them. He wasn't one for feelings, while Apollo always had been. Poetry and music were great when it came to that, but Set had been devoid of both of those for too long. With Apollo there, he had to face how he felt and what it meant, but it wasn't an easy thing.

Luckily, he wouldn't have to do it alone. Apollo would be there for him for as long as he needed help.

Apollo had wanted to talk about this before, but he'd thought it would be better to let Set focus on this situation first. He'd promised that as soon as Set was back, they'd talk, and he had every intention of following up with that promise. It might have sounded like a threat to Set, but it wasn't. Apollo just needed to know where they stood.

The sound of footsteps outside the suite made him perk up. He stopped moving and placed himself in front of the door, hoping Set had finally returned — in one piece and not wounded.

When the door opened, Apollo was relieved. Set seemed to

be fine, and his clothes were as pristine as they always were. Apollo took a step forward, but something in Set's expression stopped him.

"What happened?" he asked.

Set closed the door and leaned against it. He looked tired, which was unusual. "Apophis never came."

Apollo moved forward. "We expected him not to come." It had been a risk, but they'd had to take it. It would be stupid of Apophis to act on the information the spy had given him because he'd have to have suspected it could be a trap.

Set nodded. "Tefnut did, though. She attacked her father, and I had to stop her."

Apollo stood in front of Set, unsure what he could do to help him feel better. "I'm sorry you had to deal with that."

Set squared his jaw. "I expected it. It was just hard to watch, because it broke Ra's heart."

"I'm really sorry."

Set shrugged and pushed away from the door. "Better me than someone else."

Now wasn't the right moment to talk about them, but that didn't mean Apollo couldn't be there for Set. This might be the wrong move, but it looked like Set needed to be comforted and to feel like even though he'd done the right thing, the right thing didn't always *feel* right.

Set always behaved like he was strong and never doubted his actions, but Apollo knew that wasn't true. Deep inside, Set wanted to be accepted, and he was probably afraid that he wouldn't be. He might feel like the others would look at him with horror because of what he'd had to do.

Apollo would never look at him like that. What Set had done had needed to be done, and Apollo wanted him to know that whatever happened, he'd never feel differently.

He cupped Set's face with both hands. Set opened his mouth, probably to tell him to fuck off, but Apollo didn't give him time to do so. He leaned forward and pressed their lips together, smiling when Set gasped and opened his mouth.

Apollo pushed his tongue inside. Set needed to be distracted, and Apollo was great at distracting people. He could start singing or telling Set poetry, but this was better. They wouldn't need to talk, which was one of the things Set hated doing.

Apollo pushed Set back against the door. Set sighed, but Apollo didn't wait to see if Set would have something to say about this. He dropped to his knees and reached for Set's pants, looking up only briefly to ensure it was okay with him.

Set was watching him with an expression that made Apollo want to offer him the world. Set had been doing so much, and he'd never expected anything in exchange. He just wanted to keep his people happy.

He was making Apollo happy, and Apollo wanted him to know that.

Since Set wasn't stopping him, Apollo quickly unfastened his belt, then his pants. He grinned when he saw the boxer briefs after he let the pants drop to the floor. On the outside, Set always dressed seriously, with dark suits and shirts, but his boxers were dark green with little bananas on them.

What was even more interesting was the growing banana under them. Apollo smiled at his own stupid joke, then leaned forward to mouth Set's cock with his lips. It twitched under his touch, growing harder the longer Apollo dedicated himself to it.

"I thought you wanted to talk," Set croaked.

Apollo grinned up at him. "Well, I'm going to use my mouth, just not the way I expected."

"You don't have to do this."

"What if I want to do it?" Set wasn't used to people taking care of him, and Apollo was planning on changing that.

Starting right now.

He slid Set's boxer briefs down his legs. They joined the pants in a heap around Set's ankles while Apollo ran his palms up and down Set's legs. The skin was soft and hairy, tickling Apollo's hands.

Apollo leaned forward and licked the head of Set's cock. Set swore and bunched his hands into fists as if he was afraid to reach for Apollo. Apollo didn't mind a bit of hair-pulling, though, so he grabbed both of Set's hands and gently pulled them to his head.

He didn't have to say anything. Set's fingers dove into his curls, gently pulling him forward. Apollo obeyed the silent order and opened his mouth. He wrapped his fingers around the base of Set's cock to keep it steady, then swallowed it.

Set shouted, but he didn't let go of Apollo's head. He didn't force him into anything, though. It felt like he was anchoring himself, and that was perfectly fine with Apollo. He wanted Set to feel like he was his anchor in the storm.

He used every trick he'd ever learned, both from humans and other gods. He wanted Set to forget what had happened today and to focus on what was happening *now*, and he thought he was doing a good job. When he looked up, Set's expression had smoothed out. He didn't look worried any-more, even though Apollo knew that part of him probably was. He was focused on what Apollo was doing to him, which was what Apollo had wanted.

But maybe Set needed more. Apollo let go of his cock but stayed where he was, on his knees in front of the god he'd fallen in love with. "What do you want?"

"This is good," Set said.

Apollo shook his head. "That's not what I asked. I want to know what you *want*. I'll do pretty much anything to make you happy. I think you already know that by now."

Set sucked in a breath. "It doesn't make sense."

Apollo got to his feet and leaned over to kiss Set. "It doesn't have to make sense. Love rarely ever makes sense."

Set closed his eyes. "Is that what's happening between us? Love?"

"In time."

"I don't understand why you'd want that with me."

"You don't have to understand it."

Apollo grabbed Set's hand and pulled him toward the couch. Thankfully it wasn't far, because Set's pants and underwear were still around his ankles. He had to shuffle forward, which made Apollo laugh. Set seemed to understand that he wasn't being mean and didn't do anything beyond rolling his eyes. He was clearly just happy, and this was how he showed it.

When they reached the couch, Apollo leaned over its back and pushed his hand between the cushions to retrieve a bottle of lube. He raised it so Set could see it, and he saw the moment Set decided to give in. He pushed Apollo against the couch, and Apollo barely managed to catch himself. In this position, his ass was to Set, which sounded like the perfect way for Set to fuck him.

Apollo wiggled his butt. "You won't need to use a lot of that."

Set's free hand landed on Apollo's ass to caress it. "No?"

"You've been avoiding me, but I haven't been avoiding my dildo. In fact, we had a very nice date this morning."

Set sucked in a breath and pulled down Apollo's shorts. They were the kind with an elastic band, so he didn't have to worry about buttons. Apollo had been wearing them on purpose, and he was glad it had finally paid off.

He was also glad he wasn't wearing underwear. It gave Set easy access, which he quickly put to use.

Apollo heard the sound of the bottle of lube opening, and he waited for Set's slick fingers. They landed on his ass cheek before quickly making their way where he wanted them. Set pushed two inside, and Apollo pushed slack with pleasure.

It didn't hurt at all. He wanted more, but he didn't want to rush Set into anything. Thankfully, it didn't look like he would have to.

"You're so ready for me," Set said with a growl.

"I thought of you when I used my dildo."

Set pushed a third finger inside of Apollo. "Did you?"

"I did." Apollo sounded breathless. "I thought of how you would fuck me hard without hesitation. I don't need you to coddle me. I'm a god, and I'm strong. I can take whatever you throw at me."

Something bumped against Apollo's ass, and Apollo was sure it wasn't more fingers. It felt slick and damp. "Fuck me," he begged. He would never have a problem begging when it came to Set.

Set pulled out his fingers, which were quickly replaced by his cock. Just like Apollo had imagined, he didn't hesitate. He fucked right into him in a long smooth movement that made Apollo shout out his pleasure.

Set's fingers gripped Apollo's hips as he pounded into him. Apollo held on for dear life, but the force Set was putting into fucking him was making even the couch move.

Apollo loved it.

He took a risk and let go of the couch with one hand, reaching for his cock. Set was focused on his own pleasure, which was what Apollo had wanted. He didn't have any problems taking care of himself. He pulled on his cock, groaning when Set's cock hit his prostate. Set was long and thick, and he was filling Apollo to the brink.

Apollo loved it. He loved being stuffed, especially when it was with Set. He could hardly believe he'd get to do this anytime he wanted in the future.

Set ground his cock into Apollo, and Apollo went faster. He needed to come, and he didn't want Set to have to think about his pleasure, not right now. Thankfully, it wasn't long. He'd been yearning for this for a long time, and now that he had it, he couldn't resist the pleasure.

He whimpered as he came all over the back of the couch while Set continued to fuck him. He screwed his eyes shut and allowed Set to do whatever he wanted with him.

Set wasn't noisy when he came, but Apollo felt him shudder and press deep inside of him. It was almost as if Set wanted to go as deep as he could and become part of Apollo. Maybe he didn't understand that he was already part of Apollo's heart.

They were both panting and sweaty, and Apollo wouldn't have it any other way. He let go of the couch, flopping forward and allowing the couch to hold him up. He didn't know what Set would do now that they were done, but whatever it was, it didn't matter as long as he didn't run.

Apollo had gotten what he wanted. Set had finally fucked him.

"Everything all right?" Set asked as he stepped away.

Apollo grieved the loss of contact, but he reminded himself that it didn't have to be for long and turned around. Set looked slightly hesitant, which was so much like him it hurt Apollo's heart, so Apollo leaned forward to kiss him. "Everything's perfect."

That earned him one of Set's rare smiles, and it told Apollo that everything would be all right.

It had to be.

# CHAPTER TEN

Set almost couldn't believe this was happening. He'd been resisting Apollo long enough that it felt unreal that he'd finally given in.

Apollo's arm around Set's waist tightened, and Set turned to look at him. He was still sleeping, but then Apollo was used to sleeping in, so Set wasn't surprised.

What he was surprised about was that he was still in bed with Apollo. Once he was awake, he'd had the hardest time staying in bed. He felt like he was wasting time, but even though he wasn't doing anything, this wasn't time wasted. It was time spent with the man he was falling in love with.

It had been a few days since everything had happened with Ra and Tefnut. Ra's heart was still broken, and Set hurt for him, but he was also the happiest he'd ever been. He hadn't expected what had happened when he returned home after being in the underworld, but Apollo had been there for him, and he'd continued being there every time Set had needed him since then. Set could see the two of them working as a couple, even though he hadn't been able to before.

They might not have a chance to see what would happen if they truly became a couple. It all depended on what Apophis would do and who would die in the fight against him. For now, Apophis hadn't done anything to avenge the loss of his spy, but that was bound to change. Apophis wouldn't let it go.

Set's phone vibrated on his nightstand. It wasn't the first time that morning, but he was almost afraid of what he'd find if he answered, so he ignored it again. He realized he shouldn't have done that when he heard the main door of his suite slam open. He jerked into a sitting position, but he wasn't fast enough to get out of bed and dress. His bedroom door opened, and Ra stood there, breathing hard. He barely spared a glance for Set and Apollo, who was waking up, too. He strode toward the TV in front of the bed and turned it on.

Set scowled, but not at Ra, even though he was uncomfortable with his great-grandfather being here while he was naked with Apollo. No, his scowl was dedicated to Apophis.

*Half of New York City is now gone,* the anchor on the screen said. He was pale, and his hands shook as he tried to press them against the table.

The images behind him were horrible, but Set forced himself to look at them.

He knew New York. He had an apartment there, and he'd had an appointment with the man who made his suits, dammit. It was almost as if Apophis had known that and had decided to annoy Set.

"This is his answer," Ra said, staring at the screen. "He knows we took away his spy, and he's punishing us for it."

"We have to do something," Set said.

Ra turned toward him. His eyebrows rose on his forehead at the sight of Apollo lounging in Set's bed, but thankfully, he didn't say anything about it.

"I'm calling for a meeting," Ra said.

Set groaned. "Since when are they helpful?"

"This will be the final one. I'm done waiting. I'm done giving Apophis the opportunity to hurt more people. It's my responsibility to get rid of him, and I will."

He turned and started to leave. Set scrambled out of bed to go after him before remembering he was still naked. Apollo chuckled, so Set glared at him before rushing into the bathroom.

His heart raced. This was it. They were finally about to face Apophis.

Part of him was relieved, because he hated sitting here without doing anything and watching Apophis destroy half of the human realm. Another part of him was anxious and scared. He would never admit it to anyone, but he remembered all too well how strong Apophis had been the first time he'd fought him. If he was anywhere near that strong, it would be hard to defeat him.

But Ra was right. Apophis was hurting too many people, and it was time for them to stand up to him. If they lost, hopefully, another pantheon would step in. It would be unorthodox, but if they didn't want the human realm to be completely destroyed, they would have to do something.

Set washed up as quickly as he could before rushing out. He was relieved to see that Apollo had risen, and after a quick kiss, he went into the bathroom. By the time he was done, Set was ready to go.

He was thankful when Apollo didn't tease him about the fact that he was almost vibrating with anxiety. He just followed Set down the hallway to Ra's rooms.

They weren't the first to arrive. There was already a decent crowd there, but Set found Ra immediately. He was talking with Nu, who appeared determined.

Set sighed. He wasn't looking forward to yet another meeting, but he believed Ra when he said it would be the last one. The decisions that would be made today could mean their defeat or their victory.

He reached back and grabbed Apollo's hand, twining their fingers together. He noticed several people staring at them, but he didn't care.

He never had, and that wasn't about to change. They had better things to focus on, anyway. The fight against Apophis was coming at them quickly, and they needed to be ready.

Because Apophis would be.

Apollo was holding hands with Set. He could hardly believe it, but the proof was there, linked with his fingers. He probably looked like an idiot because he was smiling so hard, but he didn't care.

He was holding hands with Set!

Set pulled Apollo deeper into the room. Apollo realized they were headed toward Ra, so he followed easily. He didn't know what Set thought of Ra bursting in on them this morning, but so far, neither of them had said anything about it. Clearly, Set didn't have a problem with people knowing the two of them were together. He walked as if he owned the room, glaring a bit when he noticed someone staring. As far as Apollo was concerned, they were welcome to stare as much as they wanted. Yes, he'd managed to snag Set. *Go, him.*

Ra nodded when they reached him, but there was no time to talk. He turned his attention to the rest of the room and stood up straighter, his expression telling everyone how serious he was.

"I'm sure that by now you know that we found the spy. She has been taken care of, and Apophis has already taken revenge for that."

"You mean he's attacked New York because of that?" someone asked.

"I suspect that was his reason, yes. All of us are tired of his attacks. It's time to face Apophis, and no matter what happens when we do, I know that everyone here will do what they can to defeat him."

The silence in the room was almost absolute. Apollo leaned closer to Set, knowing that this was a heavy moment for everyone. It was for him, too, but he didn't know Apophis beyond what he'd seen of him over the past few months. He'd never had to deal with him before then, and he didn't know what had happened in detail. He'd always focused on what was happening now rather than on the past, but he wondered if maybe he should have looked into it.

He wasn't sure it mattered. He would be there, but he wouldn't be the one fighting Apophis. He'd tried before, and he'd failed both times. It was time to let the people who knew what they were doing do their job.

He hated that one of those people would be Set, but he wouldn't try to stop him. Set needed to do this, and Apollo would support him. He could only pray that Set made it out alive, which was odd because he was a god. He didn't pray. He was prayed to.

"When?" Osiris asked.

"He's tearing through New York right now. If we wait until that's over, he'll be more tired. We can take him on then. I wish there was more we could do for the city, but recklessly going in won't help anyone."

He didn't have to say that he hoped it meant Apophis would be more easily dealt with after spending his morning attacking a city and killing people. They might be gods, but they weren't immortal. They could be killed, and Apollo had no doubt that Apophis wouldn't hesitate to do so if he had the opportunity. Apophis wanted to be the most powerful god, and he couldn't be if he allowed other gods to survive.

Apollo suspected that had always been his plan. He was focused on the human realm now, but eventually, he would have moved on to the Egyptian pantheon and then to others. If no one was able to stop him, he would have killed all the gods to become a supreme god or something as ridiculous.

Apollo shuddered at the thought. He could think of nothing worse.

"Get ready," Ra said. "By the end of the day, this will be over."

He didn't exactly give the best pep talks, but at least he was honest. Everyone knew what they were about to face. Apophis and his demons were ransacking New York, but soon, they'd be done, and that was when Ra would attack.

Apollo swallowed. He wasn't a god of war. He could defend himself quite easily and hold his own in a fight, but he wasn't so arrogant to think that he could win against Apophis.

Well, not anymore.

He turned to Set. "You'll be careful?" he asked.

Set cocked his head. "You're not going to ask me not to do it?"

"Would it make you change your mind? You're stubborn, and you feel this is your duty. It might be. Whatever the case, you'll do this, no matter what I have to say about it. I know I won't be able to stop you, but I want at least a promise that you'll be careful."

To Apollo's surprise, Set leaned closer to kiss him. He did it in front of everyone in the room without hesitation. "How can I not be? You'll be here, waiting for me."

*Dammit.* Apollo wasn't one to cry easily, but Set was pushing him. "I won't be waiting here for you. I'll be out there fighting."

Set sighed. "I know. I wish I could convince you otherwise, but I won't try."

"Good. As long as we're clear on the fact that we'll both come back in one piece, I'm sure everything will be all right."

A loud explosion shook the palace. Apollo's eyes widened, and he looked around, wondering what it was. Part of him knew, even though no one could be sure what was going on.

"He's attacking the palace," Set said. He turned to Ra, who was rushing toward them.

"I guess New York City wasn't enough for him anymore," Apollo said.

"Be careful," Set ordered.

Apollo could only nod. When Set stepped away, he followed. He might not be able to help Set and Ra in their fight against Apophis, but he also might be, and he didn't want to risk it. Besides, he was sure that where Apophis was, his demons would be.

He raised his hands and called for his sword. It appeared in his palms, its bright light illuminating the room.

"Show off," Set muttered.

Apollo chuckled, startled by the teasing. "I'm not the one who fights with two swords," he pointed out.

Set grinned at him and raised his hands. His two swords appeared, as dark as Apollo's sword was light.

But then this was them, wasn't it? From the outside, they looked like they couldn't work. They were too different. On the inside, though, the darkness and light balanced each other. If Apollo thought about it, it made sense that Set was the person he'd fallen in love with. He was everything Apollo wasn't, but at the same time, he was everything Apollo wanted.

Apollo grabbed Set's suit jacket and pulled him close to kiss him. They didn't have time, which meant they had to keep it quick, but Set wouldn't go out there not knowing what Apollo felt for him. "Don't be an idiot and return to me. I won't lose the man I love because of Apophis."

Set's smile was pleased. "You love me?"

"As if you didn't already know that. Now go and kick his ass."

Set kissed Apollo again, then stepped away. Apollo could only watch him as he joined Ra at the door that led into the garden. They looked at each other for a second, and Ra nodded. Together, he and Set pushed open the door and stepped out.

Right into chaos.

They should have seen this coming. Apophis was annoyed and probably angry that they'd taken both Maahes and his spy from him, and he was getting revenge. What better way than to destroy the palace where the gods lived?

It hadn't been destroyed yet when Set stepped into the garden, but it would be soon if they didn't intervene. The place was crawling with demons, and more were coming out of several black barges. Set wanted to stop and kill them, but he and Ra had to climb onto Ra's solar barge. It was protected with spells that would ensure that Apophis couldn't hurt them while they fought him.

Or at least, that was the plan.

He hated leaving without helping, but when he turned, he realized he didn't have to worry. The gods who'd been supporting their fight against Apophis had already stepped out and were fighting the demons. Set even noticed gods who hadn't been involved until now stepping up and doing what was necessary. They'd finally realized they couldn't hide from this. Apophis had brought the fight to them, and they couldn't ignore it.

Ra and Set rushed toward the building where Ra's barge was kept. Set had to kill a few demons on the way there, but they got to the building without being wounded. He was tempted to look back and check in on Apollo and the others, but he couldn't.

"Is it even in a good enough state to do this?" he asked Ra as they opened the door and rushed inside.

Ra nodded. "I made sure it was. Climb in."

They did. Set swallowed hard when he stepped onto the barge. It was as he remembered — a long open span of light-colored wood with a throne in the center. He doubted Ra would be sitting anytime soon.

But the two of them weren't enough to operate the barge. They needed other gods, and while they should be arriving as they'd planned, Set wondered if he and Ra would have to do this on their own.

Thankfully, they wouldn't. More gods ran into the building, and Set sighed in relief. This was the first step in defeating Apophis.

Soon, he and Ra were surrounded. The gods had always provided a protective barrier around the boat to shield Ra from Apophis, and they would this time, too.

The barge shook under Set, then started moving. One side of the building had wide doors that burst open, and seconds later, the barge flew through the opening. The wind whipped Set's skin, but he raised his swords, ready to take on whatever was happening out there.

They took to the air. Set glanced under them, wanting to know what was happening. It looked like the demons were being held back, which was what they wanted. He tried to find Apollo, but even though Apollo was usually easy to find, there were too many people moving around. He told himself that Apollo could defend himself quite well and that it would be easy for him to fight demons. He'd had trouble against Apophis, but Apophis was incredibly strong. Demons weren't, and Set was sure that Apollo was having fun cutting heads off.

He didn't know when he'd started caring about Apollo so much, and while it still scared him, at the same time, he wouldn't have it any other way. He'd never felt like this for anyone, not even for the goddess he'd married. Apollo was the center of his world, and he wasn't sure he'd survive if something happened to him.

That was why he'd have to make sure to return to him. Apollo had told him he loved him, and Set wanted to be able to tell him that he felt the same, and not just because he thought they were going to die. He wanted to tell him so they could start a new life together.

As soon as Apophis was gone.

Set looked up, and his gaze caught Ra's. Ra's expression was grim, but he nodded at Set. "Ready?"

Set raised his swords. "As ready as I'll ever be. Do you know where he is?"

"I'm sure we'll find out soon." He hesitated. "Thank you for being here with me. I know that in the past, we haven't always seen eye to eye, but it means something to me."

Ra was talking about feelings, which made Set want to turn and run. He didn't talk about feelings. He didn't *have* feelings.

Except that wasn't true. It never had been, but now that he'd met Apollo, he couldn't deny it anymore. He couldn't ignore his feelings, either. "There's nowhere else I'd rather be."

Ra snorted. "We both know that's not true."

"Well, I'm sure you'd rather be with Frey than with me, but it'll be over soon."

"Let's hope that you're right."

Set was pretty sure he was. He didn't know what would happen, but it wouldn't last long. Apophis was done waiting. He wanted revenge, and he was here to get it.

Set and Ra's job was to stop him before he could.


Apollo's place wasn't on the barge, but he still had to resist the urge to run after Set and climb onto it. He didn't belong to this pantheon, and Set and Ra had already done this once. They knew what they were doing, and it would be better if Apollo didn't distract them.

Besides, there was plenty to do here.

Apollo raised his sword and cut off the head of a demon. Its body listed forward, and Apollo kicked it as he continued

115

moving ahead. He was surrounded by fights, but he couldn't tell who was winning just yet. The demons had numbers on their side. There were countless demons crawling all over the place, much more than they thought Apophis had managed to keep. It could become a problem, but Apollo would make sure it didn't.

Besides, he wasn't the only one fighting. Everyone around him was busy doing the same, cutting demons' heads off and stabbing them. All the gods had manifested weapons and were using them in a way that told Apollo they knew what they were doing. Even Nu, whom Apollo couldn't have imagined in a fight before, was holding their own. In fact, they were pretty impressive. They were wielding two spears, using them to stab any demon that came close enough.

A screech made Apollo jump, and he turned, ready to use his sword. His eyes widened when he saw that he wouldn't need to.

Barnaby was riding on the back of one of the demons, hitting the demon's head with what looked like a metal plate. It wouldn't do him much good, but the demon didn't seem to know how to get him off its back, and while he was trying, it wasn't succeeding. Lance was in front of the demon, throwing stones at the demon's head and effectively distracting it.

Laughter bubbled out of Apollo's chest. He was sure they would win this now. He just had to look at the two humans to know. They didn't have to be here. In fact, Apollo was pretty sure the plan had been for them to stay in the palace and hide. Instead, they were fighting in any way they could. They couldn't manifest weapons, but they'd found objects that would help them, and they were using them creatively.

Apollo moved forward and slashed his sword down toward the demon's legs. He cut the demon at both ankles. The demon roared and raised its sword, but as it tried to turn toward Apollo, it tilted forward. Apollo offered Barnaby a hand, and Barnaby took it, allowing Apollo to help him climb off the demon.

The demon crashed to the ground, and Lance was on it right away. He'd found a bigger stone, and he smashed it against the demon's head. The demon attempted to crawl away, but without the use of its legs, it wouldn't go far.

Apollo let go of Barnaby's hand and stepped forward. Lance blinked at him and quickly scrambled back, giving Apollo the space he needed to cut the demon's head off. It was satisfying to see the head roll sideways.

When Apollo turned back to Barnaby, Barnaby looked a little green. He was clutching the metal plate against his chest and staring at the demon's head.

Apollo kicked it into a bush so Barnaby wouldn't have to see it anymore. It probably wouldn't help much, since the garden was full of bodies and body parts, but at least Barnaby wouldn't have to look at this one.

"Are you all right?" Apollo asked.

"We're fine," Lance answered.

Apollo wasn't sure he believed them, but then, he wasn't sure anyone was fine at the moment.

He manifested two short swords and held them out to the two humans by the blades. "Use these. They'll be more useful than a plate and a few stones."

Lance took his right away, but Barnaby eyed the sword as if it might bite him. "I don't know. I don't want to cut off my own toes."

Apollo grinned. "I'm sure Thoth would love you even without toes. He can only love you if you're still here, though, and that metal plate isn't going to help you for long. You can take the sword, but you can also return to the palace. I can help you find a safe space to hide."

Barnaby shook his head. "I'm not going anywhere."

Apollo wondered if the two had talked to their partners

about this. He doubted Osiris and Thoth would have agreed to have their human lovers fight like this, but they were nowhere to be seen, which meant it fell on Apollo to protect Lance and Barnaby. He couldn't force them to retreat, but he could make sure they had a better chance at winning the fights they took on.

Barnaby finally let go of the plate and took the sword. He looked surprised when he raised it, then swung it a few times. "It's lighter than I thought."

"I didn't want to burden either of you with a heavy sword." Apollo hesitated. He didn't want to think about this possibility, but he couldn't avoid it. "You won't be able to use these if I die. They'll vanish. If that happens, find a safe place to hide, please."

Barnaby glared at Apollo and, to his surprise, threw himself into his arms. Apollo was still holding his sword, so he had to be careful, but he managed to grab Barnaby and hug him back.

"You're not gonna die," Barnaby ordered.

"I plan to stay alive, but I don't know what might happen."

"*I* know. You'll fight, and you'll win. When this is over, we can gossip about Set and how he is in bed. You know the answer to that now, don't you?"

Apollo grinned. "I do. I'll give you all the gritty details as long as you make it out of this fight."

"I will." Barnaby sounded determined, and Apollo hoped he was right.

He saw something move above him and looked up. The barge, carrying Apollo and Ra, cut through the sky and looked almost as bright as the sun. It reminded Apollo of his chariot. He kind of wanted to be on it right now, but that wasn't his fight. It was best for him to focus on the demons.

But part of his heart was on that barge. He knew where it was going, and he couldn't help but want to go with it.

He patted Barnaby's back and gently pushed him away. "Be careful."

Barnaby nodded. His expression was set, and Apollo was sure that he would start chopping off demon body parts as soon as he had one close enough. He wished he could see him in action, but even though he wasn't on the barge, he didn't want to be far from it.

He left Lance and Barnaby behind and ran after the barge.

# CHAPTER ELEVEN

It wasn't the first time Set and Ra had fought side-by-side, but it had been a while. Set wasn't surprised to feel like no time had passed, though. The two of them still moved seamlessly, cutting down demons who tried to crawl onto the barge while looking for Apophis at the same time.

He wouldn't be hiding, but he also wasn't in plain sight. It made Set wonder what he was up to. He was probably watching from afar and waiting for the right moment to attack Ra, taking pleasure in what his demons were doing. Set had to resist the urge to look down many times. Being up high meant he'd have a perfect view of what was happening at the palace, but he was afraid of what he'd see.

What if they'd lost people who were part of their family? There were gods whom Set wouldn't care if they died or lived, but he cared very much about Apollo, Lance, Barnaby, and the others.

He cut down a demon and pushed it off the barge, then leaned down to look. They weren't very high, but it still took him a moment to realize what he was looking at.

*Where had Barnaby found a sword?*

The human was gleefully hacking at a demon, which Set hadn't expected. Barnaby and Lance were supposed to be hiding in the palace, so why were they out there, cutting demons to pieces? They had to work together because they weren't strong enough to take down a demon on their own, but they were doing a good job, which was surprising.

Set squinted and looked at the swords they were using.

They were so bright that he didn't have to wonder where they'd gotten them for long.

*Apollo.*

Osiris and Thoth were going to be pissed, but the sight made Set smile. Of course Apollo had wanted to be sure that his friends could defend themselves. It was the kind of person he was. He loved his people, and he did what he could for them.

A sword appeared in Set's vision, and he twirled around, pressing his back against the railing of the barge. The sword landed against the railing with a thwack, and when the demon tried to pull it out, it couldn't because it was stuck. Set grinned and raised his swords. He killed the demon quickly before pushing it away and turning. Ra was finishing off another demon, and they looked at each other when it fell to the ground. More were crawling up on the sides of the barge.

"We have to find him," Ra called out.

Set nodded and leaned over the railing to check the garden and the palace. Where was Apophis hiding?

He followed the direction from which the demons were coming to try to find the source. He'd noticed only one black barge earlier, but there were more now. The demons had needed a way to get to the palace, and there were too many of them for Apophis to teleport them. He'd used barges, but he'd be alone on his. It would also probably be the biggest one.

Set grinned when he found it. It wasn't close to the palace, but there was no mistaking it for the other ones. It was massive, made of glistening black wood and decorated with gold.

"There," he said, pointing his finger toward the barge.

Ra nodded, and their barge started moving in that direction. Set sucked in a breath. The hardest fight was about to start.

He had a few seconds before they reached Apophis, so he quickly took off his suit jacket. He rolled up the sleeves of his shirt, then readied his swords again.

He was as ready as he would ever be.

"Apophis," Ra called out when they were close enough.

Apophis looked up. He was standing on his barge, watching his demons wreak havoc on the palace. He and Set looked alike. They both had long black hair and dark eyes and wore black suits. Thankfully, his heart wasn't as dark as Apophis's. He might be the god of violence, but he'd never wanted destruction like Apophis did. He'd only ever wanted to be left in peace, and Apophis had made that impossible.

He would pay for that.

Apophis smiled. He was a handsome man, but his eyes were cold like a snake's. The smile didn't make him any more handsome. It made him look like a cobra ready to strike.

Set called on his power and manifested spears that he threw toward Apophis. Apophis's eyes widened for just a second, and he raised his hand, deflecting several of them.

But not all of them.

One of the spears hit Apophis's thigh. Set couldn't see blood because the clothes Apophis was wearing were black, but he knew he'd hit him.

He grinned. He'd wounded Apophis, making him weaker. He'd still have a lot of strength, but this would make it easier for them to defeat him.

Apophis pulled the spear out of his thigh and threw it to the side. Set had known that defeating him wouldn't be easy, so he wasn't surprised. He was ready to fight.

As soon as the barges were close enough, Set jumped off theirs and onto Apophis's. Demons rushed him, but he cut them down even as he worked on making new spears. He threw all of them toward Apophis, hoping to distract him while Ra attacked him.

Once more gods arrived to help with the demons, Set turned his attention to Apophis. He and Ra were locked in a fight, their swords moving quickly. Set didn't want to distract Ra, but he might have to help. He had last time, and while Ra might be able to take on Apophis by himself this time around, why should he have to? Set was there, ready to help.

Apophis took a step back and stumbled onto an arm. He quickly got his feet under him, but Set took advantage of that moment to create another spear and throw it at Apophis's back. Apophis twisted his upper body just in time and met the spear with his sword, pushing it away, which gave Ra the opportunity to swing forward.

Apophis hissed when Ra's sword penetrated his stomach. It wouldn't be enough to kill him, but if he couldn't focus on healing himself, he would have a hard time winning this fight. If they could keep him distracted long enough, they'd be able to subdue him.

Apophis surged forward with his sword, pushing Ra away. Just then, three demons attacked Ra from behind. Set rushed forward to help him, and while it didn't take them more than a few minutes, by the time they turned back to Apophis, he was on the other side of the barge. He was running away, probably to give himself time to heal, but they couldn't allow that to happen. The fight needed to end today.

A flash of gold made Set look up. His eyes widened when he saw that Apollo had appeared out of nowhere and was cutting off Apophis's path to safety. He raised his sword and grinned like the idiot he was, even winking at Set when he saw him watching.

"Where do you think you're going?" Apollo asked Apophis.

Apophis snarled and raised his sword, but Apollo caught it with his. There was a clash of darkness and light so bright that Set had to close his eyes.

When he opened them again, it was to find Apollo and Apophis fighting. Apophis was bleeding heavily, but that didn't seem to slow him down. Apollo was still smiling, looking like he was having the time of his life.

Set sucked in a breath when Apophis's sword came too close to Apollo's neck. Apollo danced out of the way, but Set's heart raced.

That idiot was going to get himself killed. How could he do that when he'd made Set fall in love with him?

Apollo was the most infuriating god — the most infuriating *person* — Set had ever met, but he'd fallen for him with all his heart, and he wouldn't allow anyone to hurt him, not even Apollo himself. He was doing what he felt was right, not thinking about his own safety, and Set would make sure to yell at him for that once they were alone.

He twirled his swords in his hands and looked at Ra, who nodded grimly.

Before Set could yell at Apollo, they needed to defeat Apophis.


Apollo knew he wouldn't win this fight, but he'd never intended to. He was attacking Apophis to slow him down and give Set and Ra the opportunity to reach them. They couldn't allow Apophis to escape, which meant someone had to stop him.

Clearly, that someone was Apollo.

His sword clashed with Apophis's, and Apollo stumbled back. He pushed forward again without hesitation, knowing that if Apophis killed him, Set would avenge him. He'd rather not allow Apophis to kill him, but he wasn't sure he'd have a choice if he continued the fight.

"What the fuck are you thinking?" Set bellowed as he rushed toward Apollo and Apophis.

Apollo kept his gaze on Apophis. He was dangerous, with his body coiled like a snake waiting to strike. When Apollo swung his sword sideways, Apophis raised his, stopping it. Apollo launched forward, hitting Apophis from the left, then from the right before jumping back. Apophis managed to counter all the attacks, but it wouldn't stop Apollo, especially when help was coming so quickly.

He noticed movement behind Apophis and grinned. Set had arrived, with Ra right behind him, which meant that Apollo was safe. He'd managed to survive a third fight with Apophis, and he was pretty sure it was a record.

But his smile betrayed that something was happening. As Set raised his swords to attack Apophis, Apophis turned and slashed at him with his sword. Ra grabbed Set's shirt and pulled him back, but not quickly enough. Blood bloomed on Set's white shirt, and Apollo almost dropped his sword from shock. For a second, he could have sworn that time stopped moving.

Set's expression didn't falter, even though he had to be in pain. Apollo expected him to attack Apophis with his swords, and it looked like Apophis felt the same. He shifted forward, ready to stop Set's attack.

A spear appeared behind Apophis. Apollo sucked in a breath, getting Apophis's attention, but it was too late. The spear went through him, aimed at his heart. He stumbled back and reached for the spear with his free hand. He wrapped bloody fingers around it and pulled, and Apollo wondered if he could survive this. He wouldn't have been surprised if it took more than that to kill Apophis, but thankfully, he wouldn't have to worry about Apophis surviving. Set raised both of his swords and slashed them down.

Apophis's eyes widened in shock. His mouth opened, and blood gurgled out, which made Apollo wrinkle his nose. He really could have done without the gore. It would take a while to clean up. Thankfully, they were on Apophis's barge, so maybe they could just set everything on fire and call it a day.

Apophis's head slid forward. His body stayed upright for a few more seconds before following it to the floor of the barge. It crumpled like a marionette with cut ropes, and Apollo stared at the powerful god who'd tried to erase humanity.

"That's it?" he asked.

Set snorted. "Of course you're not even a little bit impressed. I just killed Apophis, but it's not enough for you."

"I remember how hard it was to fight with him, but I expected this to be harder. We've been talking about it for weeks."

Set rolled his eyes and lowered his swords. "Only because Ra wanted to plan this to the second."

He vanished one of the swords and reached for his chest, where more blood was seeping from his wound. Apollo rushed forward, wanting to check on him, almost stabbing him with his sword when he reached him.

"Don't put it away," Set ordered as Apollo was about to do just that. "Apophis might be gone, but his demons are still here, and we need to get rid of every last one of them."

Apollo looked at Ra, who was shaking his head. He was glad to see he and the other sun god had the same opinion on Set going back to fighting when he was hurt.

"You're wounded," Ra said as he squeezed Set's shoulder. "Let Apollo take care of you."

Set shook away Ra's hand. "I'm fine, and I have no problems killing more demons."

"You just killed Apophis. You saved us all, and you avoided an outright war during which most of the human realm and our pantheon would have died. Take a few minutes to rest, Set. No one expects you to go after demons in your state."

"Besides, our friends are doing a pretty good job of it," Apollo pointed out.

Set's eyes narrowed. "Are you talking about Barnaby and Lance? I thought they were supposed to stay inside the palace and hide?"

Apollo grinned and shrugged. "I couldn't lock them up in a room against their will, could I? They were fighting the demons with stones, Set. *Stones*. What should I have done? I gave them swords because it would keep them safer. Were they using them?"

Set shoulders slumped. "They were. Barnaby especially seemed to be having the time of his life."

Apollo wished he could have seen that, but he supposed he would see the result later. He'd have to congratulate Barnaby on a job well done.

That was, if he and Lance were still alive.

Maybe it was time for Apollo to leave the barge and go help their friends. He couldn't do so without taking care of Set first, though.

"I'll check in on everyone," Ra said as he stepped toward the edge of the barge. He glanced one last time at Apophis's body before jumping down without looking back.

Apollo pushed Apophis's head away with his toes. The god was as beautiful in death as he'd been in life, but the sight of him made Apollo shudder in horror, especially because Apophis was looking up at him. Well, his dead eyes were.

He used his foot to turn Apophis's head around so it wouldn't be staring at him. When he looked up, it was to find Set's gaze on him. Apollo gave him a winning smile, but Set's expression stayed dire.

"You killed the bad guy," Apollo said. "That's cause for celebration, but you don't look like you want to celebrate."

"That's because I'm tempted to strangle you instead."

Apollo snorted and gently poked at the wound on Set's chest. Set hissed, but he didn't pull away when Apollo lifted one side of his shirt to check the wound.

"What the fuck were you thinking?" Set asked. "He could have killed you. You put yourself in danger needlessly, even after you promised you'd be careful."

Apollo wasn't a god of medicine, but one of his sons was. Apollo had learned a few things over the years, and while he couldn't fully heal Set's wound, he could at least make sure it didn't continue bleeding.

He pressed his palm against Set's chest and focused on his power. Set was still glaring at him by the time he was done, so Apollo leaned forward and kissed his cheek.

"I won't apologize for doing what I had to do. I saw Apophis running, and I knew I had to stop him. I also knew that you would get to us before he could hurt me."

Set caught Apollo's wrist and pulled him close to kiss him on the lips. "It was still too dangerous," he muttered.

"Probably, but I'm not the one who got stabbed."

"Not this time, anyway," Set grumbled. "Besides, I didn't get stabbed. He just slashed me."

"Saying it differently doesn't change what happened."

"It's not the same. Stabbing means that your blade penetrates the body. His never did."

Apollo was aware of that, but he liked distracting Set. He smiled as Set continued to ramble, and while he wished that the fight was over, they weren't done yet. The demons wouldn't take care of themselves, unfortunately, which meant Apollo and Set needed to get back to work.

He kissed Set to shut him up, then grinned at Set's scandalized expression. "You can talk my ears off as much as you want once this is over, but let's take care of the demons first, all right?"

"Yeah, all right," Set said with pink cheeks.

Apollo looked down at Apophis's body. "What are we supposed to do with him? He can't come back from that, can he?"

"Not even gods can come back from having their head cut

off," Set confirmed. "But I'll take care of the body. I have a plan."

Apollo grabbed Set's hand and pulled him toward the edge of the barge. "Can it wait? I have demons to skewer."

"You make it sound like fun."

"That's because it is. Besides, think about it. Once we're done killing all these demons, we won't have to think about fighting for a while."

Set groaned. "Please don't say it out loud. I don't want to give anyone weird ideas."

Apollo winked at him and turned to jump off the barge, but Set stopped him and pulled him back. For a moment, he just stared at Apollo, and even though Apollo wanted to ask him what was up, he found what little patience he had and waited. He didn't want to make Set uncomfortable, and it was clear that Set had something to tell him.

For once in his life, Apollo kept his mouth shut.

They'd done it. Set and Apollo had faced Apophis and had survived the fight.

Set hadn't wanted to tell Apollo that he loved him just because he was afraid he wouldn't get another chance to do so, but he didn't have to worry about that anymore. Besides, his feelings wouldn't change, no matter what situation they were in. He'd fallen in love, and even though it made him uncomfortable, he'd come to realize there was no getting rid of the feeling.

There was no getting rid of *Apollo*, and while that might have annoyed Set before, it didn't now. Instead, it made his chest feel tight and his cheeks flush.

Set disliked feeling vulnerable and showing his emotions, but he and Apollo were alone on the barge. They could still hear screeches and the sound of people running around under them, but here on Apophis's black barge, it felt like they were alone in the world. They might as well have been. They were having a peaceful moment in the middle of a fight that could have taken out the entire palace—and maybe the entire human world.

"I wanted to tell you something," Set finally managed to say.

Apollo's smile was gentle. "You can tell me whatever you want." He paused and cocked his head. It was as if he could read Set's thoughts and knew what Set wanted to tell him. "And you don't have to tell me anything now. You can take your time. In fact, you *should* take your time."

But Set was already shaking his head. He was done waiting and finding excuses. "You told me that you love me, and I want you to know that I feel the same. I love you, too."

Apollo's smile was brighter than the sun.

It bewildered Set to realize that he'd made the sun god smile like that. It didn't feel like anything he could do or say could make someone so happy, but the proof was right in front of him.

Apollo hooked his arms around Set's neck and pulled him close to kiss him. The wound on Set's chest burned, but Set didn't make a sound. He didn't want Apollo to realize that he was in pain, and he didn't want the kiss to end.

Something slammed against the bottom of the barge, rocking it. Set swore and clung to Apollo, but Apollo kissed his cheek and gently pulled away.

"We'll have all the time in the world to do that later. We should go and see what happened. I wouldn't want the barge to be shot down with us on it."

"I don't think that's what happened," Set said as he leaned over the railing to look down at the barge.

A demon was pinned there with two spears, one in each shoulder. The thing was trying to get free while Nu watched it from the ground, smiling gleefully. They noticed Set and waved at him, and to his own surprise, he waved back.

He didn't think he'd waved at anyone in his entire life, and he wasn't sure what had pushed him to do it. It felt ridiculous, but at the same time, it was clear he'd made his grandparent happy.

"Nu is having fun," Apollo commented.

For a few moments, he and Set both stared at the demon as it wiggled. It had to hurt, since the only thing holding it up was the spears, but it didn't seem to care.

"You should go down there," Set said.

"What about you? What are you going to do?"

Set looked down at Apophis's body. It wasn't a pleasant sight, but Apophis looked human now that he was dead. There were no traces of the power he'd used to kill so many. There were also no signs of the darkness that had seeped through his every pore.

"He can't come back from this, but I want to make sure, just in case."

"What are you thinking of?"

"I'm going to cut him into pieces and have gods take them all over the world to burn them and bury the ashes. They won't tell anyone where they did so."

"That feels a bit overkill, but you know better than me. Let's do it."

Apollo hadn't said anything when Set had tortured Maahes, but he hadn't been there to see it. What would he think of Set when he saw him hack a body to pieces?

It wasn't like Set was looking forward to it, but he felt it was necessary. He wasn't taking any chances. He'd heard about stupid humans trying to revive dead gods and some-times succeeding. He wasn't willing to risk it, and this felt like the safest way to get rid of Apophis. His body would be in pieces, and each piece would be burned. There would be no coming back from that.

Hopefully.

Set shouldn't have worried about Apollo's reaction to his plan. Set had barely managed to call back his two swords when Apollo was already hacking at Apophis's body. He seemed to be particularly gleeful, reminding Set of what he'd seen Barnaby do earlier. There was a reason these two were friends, and Set shuddered in horror at the thought of what they'd be up to now that their world would be peaceful again. With no Apophis around, they would be able to focus on their friendship, and Set could already imagine the kind of trouble they'd get into.

He didn't mind. He wanted Apollo to be happy. That was the only way he'd get to keep the sun god, and he planned to do precisely that. Apollo wasn't going anywhere. He was Set's, just like Set was his.

Apollo looked up. "Well, are you going to make me do all the hard work on my own?"

Set almost said yes because it would mean he could watch Apollo, but instead he stepped forward. "Let's do this quickly. The sooner it's over, the better I'll feel."

It was a grim job, but they did it together. It made Set feel a little bit better. He didn't feel guilty about killing Apophis or cutting him into pieces, but he hated that Apollo had seen him in this kind of situation. Luckily, it didn't seem like Apollo cared.

By the time they were done, both of them were bloody and panting slightly. Set was done with the day, but it wasn't over yet.

He looked down over the railing of the barge, relieved to see that most of the demons were dead or on the run. They wouldn't be going far, because the gods seemed to have decided that not even one of them should survive.

Set agreed with that. He supposed he could have asked

Osiris to take them back to the underworld, but what would be the point? The underworld would spawn new demons anyway.

The demon that had been speared to the barge was missing its head now. Set didn't know what to do with the black barge, but he thought that burning it to ashes would be a good idea, especially with all the blood. They wouldn't even have to take down the demon if they chose that option.

"What now?" Apollo asked as he leaned next to Set. "It looks like this is pretty much over."

The fight was over, anyway. The cleanup would take time, and there would be some rebuilding to do, but at the moment, Set couldn't care less. He wrapped an arm around Apollo's waist and pulled him close. They leaned their heads together and looked down as the last of demons were caught and killed.

Set sucked in a breath. They'd done it. They had defeated Apophis, even though they hadn't believed they could do so. His chest burned, but he'd be all right, and it looked like Apollo was pretty much intact. He was sweaty and bloody, but none of the blood was his.

Set would still check every inch of his body, just in case.

"You're still up there?" Ra called out from under the barge.

Set and Apollo looked at each other. When Apollo nodded, Set took his hand and pulled him off the barge. They fell, but thankfully, it wasn't far, and Set teleported them just before they hit the ground. When they reappeared, Apollo rolled his eyes. "Show off. That fall wouldn't have killed us."

"You have to remember that I'm wounded."

"Oh, now you remember that you're wounded? I thought you were fine?"

"What did you do up there?" Ra asked as he looked at the barge. "Is that your work?"

Set looked at the headless demon and shook his head.

"That would be Nu."

Ra chuckled. "I can imagine that. Well? What happened to you? Are you more hurt than I realized?"

"No. Apollo and I cut the body into pieces. I want every piece to be taken away by a different god who won't ever tell anyone where they went. Then they'll burn their pieces and bury the ashes."

Ra nodded, his expression serious now. "We'll make sure he doesn't return."

They'd better because Set wasn't doing this a third time.

# EPILOGUE

Set was always adorable, but Apollo knew he didn't want to hear that word referred to him. How could he deny it, though, especially right now?

Apollo stared at the big black dog hiding in the bush. If Set thought that Apollo couldn't see him, he was wrong, but Apollo liked playing with Set, so he behaved as if he had no idea where his boyfriend was.

He hadn't expected Set to be so free with his affection. He gave Apollo pretty much everything he wanted, so when Apollo had declared that he was bored and wanted to play in the gardens, Set had dragged him there right away. When Apollo had told him that he'd looked into him and knew he could shift into a black dog, he'd explained that he wasn't a dog before shifting to show him.

Apollo could see the differences between Set's animal and dogs, but for lack of a better word, that was what he was calling Set. The fact that Set disliked it meant that Apollo would continue calling him a dog for the rest of their lives together.

Hopefully, they would be endless.

Set pounced, suddenly bursting out of the bush. He hit Apollo's legs and almost took both of them down to the ground, so Apollo leaned over and hauled him into his arms. He was massive, and Apollo made sure to hold him under his armpits so that his back legs dragged on the ground. He could have carried him differently, but he knew this would annoy Set.

Apollo rubbed his nose against Set's black one and smiled.

"Who's a good puppy?"

Set shifted instantly, and Apollo found himself with an armful of annoyed god.

"I'm not a puppy," Set said.

"You might not be one, but you were playing around like one."

Once, Set would have completely closed off and stormed away. He wouldn't have allowed anyone to tell him that he was playing around like a puppy. Things were different now. Apollo and Set were together, and while Set acted like he was irritated, he wasn't. Apollo had learned to read his boyfriend's body language, and he could tell that Set was pleased.

He rubbed their noses together again, and this time, they both had human noses, which meant it was less wet and cold.

"Stop that," Set argued, but he didn't push Apollo away.

"Why would I? You're adorable when you blush."

"I'm never adorable. I'm a dangerous god, and you should remember that."

"I'll remember it when I'm fucking you in the shower later," Apollo murmured.

Set cheeks went so red that Apollo wouldn't have been surprised if his head exploded. He laughed, then kissed Set's cheek. "Come on. You know you love it when I tease you."

"There's a fine line between love and hate."

Apollo laughed again and went to stretch out on one of the chairs on the lawn. He loved the sky palace and called it that because it bothered Set. He'd heard Barnaby and Lance refer to the palace that way, and it made sense. It was a palace, and it was in the sky.

But this place was nothing like Mount Olympus. There, everything was cold and hard marble. Even Apollo's throne was like that, and it hurt his butt every time he had to sit on it. He hadn't been back since he told his father to fuck off and that he was about to get involved in the fight against Apophis, and he wasn't planning on ever going back.

Set flopped into the chair next to Apollo's and reached for him. He linked their hands together, and, like always, it made Apollo's heart race. He could hardly believe that Set was comfortable enough to do this in a place where anyone could see them.

He sighed in pleasure. This was the life he'd wanted all along. He didn't have to deal with his father or the rest of their messy pantheon anymore. He'd moved permanently into the sky palace, and he wasn't planning on going anywhere anytime soon. His father had tried summoning him a few times, but Apollo had sent him a message that he was officially an Egyptian god now. It was bullshit, but he would've paid to see the explosion in the throne room when his father had gotten the message. He hoped he'd been clear. He was never going back, and if his father wanted to see him, he would have to come to him.

It would never happen. It was both a relief and sad, but Apollo had gotten over the disappointment a long time ago. He didn't need anyone from his old pantheon. He had more than enough people who cared about him here.

"Are both of you dressed?" a voice called out.

Apollo turned to see Barnaby and Lance walking toward them, both of them covering their eyes. Barnaby kept peeking from between his fingers, and he looked disappointed when he realized that both Apollo and Set were fully dressed.

"They are," he muttered.

Lance dropped his hand and looked at his friend. "How do you know? You weren't supposed to peek."

"How? There was a chance that Set was naked."

Set growled, making both of them jump. Apollo playfully whacked Set's chest, careful of the place where Apophis had wounded him. It had long healed, but it still made Apollo's stomach churn when he thought about it.

That kind of wound wouldn't have killed Set, but it had still been too close for Apollo's taste. What if Apophis's sword had been higher and nicked Set in the throat? What if Ra hadn't pulled Set away quickly enough? Set wouldn't be here today, which wasn't something Apollo wanted to think about.

"Well, neither of us is naked, which I agree is a pity," Apollo said. "If it was up to me, Set would have to walk around the palace with no clothes on every day."

"I can still change my mind," Set said in a calm voice. "I don't have to be with him. I can chalk it up to a moment of madness and go on my way."

Apollo patted Set's knee. "Look at how cute you are, talking to yourself."

"I'm not cute," Set grumbled.

"I beg to differ. You are *extremely* cute, and I'm lucky you chose me."

That seemed to mollify Set, and he leaned over to kiss Apollo as Lance and Barnaby sat down on the lawn next to the chairs.

Set glanced at them. "Don't you have anything better to do?"

"We don't," Barnaby said gleefully. "We were inside, but I think Ra had enough of us and told us to come and find you."

"He probably hoped I would kill you," Set said.

Once, Barnaby and Lance would have been afraid of him. Today, they both rolled their eyes, which made Apollo laugh.

Set crossed his arms over his chest. "Why is no one afraid of me anymore?"

"Why should they be afraid of you? They know you would never hurt them."

"He's right," Barnaby said. "We saw how worried you were about us after the fight, and we realized that you consider us part of your family just as much as Osiris and Thoth.

You wouldn't kill family. You wouldn't even torture us."

"I might change my mind about that," Set muttered.

Apollo leaned back in his chair. He watched as Barnaby and Set bickered and wondered how his father couldn't see there was nothing wrong with humans. Mount Olympus was reserved for gods, and Apollo's father would pitch a fit if anyone tried to sneak in their human lovers. The Egyptian pantheon was completely different. Everywhere Apollo looked, there were humans and gods from other pantheons. They felt like a real family, which was what he'd been looking for all along.

He hadn't thought he'd ever have one, but he'd been wrong. His family was right here, all of them safe and sound and looking forward to a bright future.

In Apollo's case, it would be a little dark because that was how Set was, but he didn't mind.

# ABOUT THE AUTHOR

Catherine is the creator of several series, most of them paranormal, including the Whitedell Pride Series and the Gillham Pack Series. While she graduated in translation, she decided to go the writer's way because it was more fun to create her own stories and characters.

She's been living in Italy for more than twenty years, but she's a daughter of the North—Belgium to be precise—and she misses it so much that she's already planning to move back.

She loves pizza—probably too much —her son, her pets, and of course, books. She sneaks some reading time into her schedule every time she has five minutes free from writing, demands from her various pets and son, and lastly, housework.

Connect with her:

lievens.catherine@gmail.com
BookBub:       https://www.bookbub.com/authors/catherine-lievens
Website: https://authorcatherinelievens.com/
Facebook:          https://www.facebook.com/catherine.lievens.9
Facebook       Group:          https://www.facebook.com/groups/411788002341528/
Twitter: https://twitter.com/authorCLievens
Newsletter: http://eepurl.com/c-uvKn